"YOU FOUND A GUN?"

"Yes," El said and pulled the gun out of his pocket.

"So you picked it up."

"Of course."

"I suppose you handled it with your bare hands?"

"Of course, I wasn't wearing gloves."

"Were you wearing gloves when you shot him?" Deputy Nelson asked.

El felt like ice water had been poured down his back.

BAPTISM BY MURDER

JAN MAXWELL

AVON BOOKS ◤◢ NEW YORK

BAPTISM BY MURDER is an original publication of Avon Books. This work has never before appeared in book form. This work is a novel. Any similarity to actual persons or events is purely coincidental.

AVON BOOKS
A division of
The Hearst Corporation
1350 Avenue of the Americas
New York, New York 10019

Copyright © 1995 by J. Maxine Jenks
Published by arrangement with the author
Library of Congress Catalog Card Number: 95-94190
ISBN: 0-380-77621-9

First Avon Books Printing: September 1995

AVON TRADEMARK REG. U.S. PAT. OFF. AND IN OTHER COUNTRIES, MARCA REGISTRADA, HECHO EN U.S.A.

Printed in the U.S.A.

RA   10   9   8   7   6   5   4   3   2   1

▲1▼

FRANKENSTEIN'S MONSTER, I'M *baptizing Franken-stein's monster.* El tried to erase that thought as Tom Rivers waded toward him, but Tom's size and slow, jerky moves fit the image too well. *Dear Lord, I'm sorry, that's wrong. He's a good man, just afraid of the water. I'm his minister and about to baptize...* El tried to suppress the thought, but it was no use. It came again. *Frankenstein's monster. No, no, Tom Rivers.*

El focused on Tom's face trying to shift his thoughts. That face matched the off-white of the baptismal robe. El smiled, he hoped reassuringly. Tom's eyes met his, prey's eyes mesmerized by his hunter.

Well, Tom warned me he was afraid of water. "Why, Lord do the big ones have to be the ones that don't want to be dunked?" he asked silently. There was no answer as usual, so he said a short prayer. "Dear Lord, help me to make this a meaningful time for him and ease his fear. Amen."

Tom was even with El now. The water was a little over waist deep, just right for most adults but not for Frankenstein's monster. El suppressed the desire to giggle. His plea to God had not helped. El went over the baptismal procedure in his head, just as he had gone over it with Tom. There should be no problem. Tom was six-four, but El was only three inches shorter. However, standing beside Tom's bulk, El felt scrawny.

El smiled again, nodded and place his hand on Tom's back. Tom's muscles were as tight as the steel cables on the Loop 360 bridge. El patted his back lightly. Tom did not relax.

El looked at the congregation. All eyes seemed to be fixed on him. *Of course, you idiot,* he said to himself, *you're the pastor. Now don't say Frankenstein's monster or you will end your career here and now,* El told himself.

"It is a great honor to get to baptize Brother Tom. I know you all appreciate the courage it takes for an adult to come forward for baptism. He's showing his commitment to Christ, it's up to all of us to help him grow in the faith."

El turned to Tom. "Have you accepted Jesus Christ as your savior?"

Tom nodded and said hoarsely, "Yes."

"Bend your knees," El whispered.

Tom bent his knees as instructed. El started to lower him backward into the water. The man was heavy. Tom's foot slipped. Suddenly, El had all Tom's weight. He could not hold him. El realized they were both going down. He gasped, "I baptize you, Thomas Raymond Rivers, in the name of the Father, Son, and Holy Spirit" just as the water closed over his head.

Somehow, both he and Tom got to their feet without too much splashing. At least the congregation had the goodness not to laugh. A few members looked as if it was hurting them not to, but none broke down, probably because of Tom. He was shivering so hard the water rippled; still, he tried to apologize to El. El hushed him and got him to the steps out of the baptistry. Otis Wheeler, one of the deacons, was at the top to help Tom out.

Tom was the last to be baptized today. "Thank God," El said under his breath. He was soaked. He wore waders to protect his clothes, but they didn't help if you fell. He nodded to Steve to start the next hymn while he struggled out of the water. Things weren't too difficult until he reached the top two steps, then he realized his waders had filled with water. He lifted pounds of water with each step. Somehow he staggered out.

Bless Brother Otis. Otis was back at the top of the steps to help him. There was not even a twinkle of laughter in Otis's eyes as he helped him to the shower stall and then to strip off his waders. Despite Otis's help, some water escaped and gushed out on the dressing room floor. Otis threw towels on the floor to soak it up.

Tom Rivers poked his head around the partition. "I'm sure sorry, pastor."

El shook his head. "It wasn't your fault. The bottom of the baptistry is pretty slick. Just get dressed and join your family." El chuckled. "You really got dunked."

Tom ducked his head, then raised it and grinned back. "So did you."

"That I did." El turned to Otis as Tom's head disappeared. "Otis, what am I going to do? I've got a change of pants, but not a shirt. I can't put my coat on over this wet shirt."

Otis nodded. "Just wait, Pastor, I'll be right back." He pattered away.

To himself, El muttered, "You should know better. Always bring a complete change of clothes on baptism day." However, this was the first time he had ever gone down with a convert.

Otis returned in a moment with a white shirt. "Wear my dress shirt, Preacher. I'll keep my suit coat on."

"Otis, I can't do that."

"Sure, you can, Pastor."

El looked into Otis's eyes, there was no glimmer of laughter, only concern.

So El delivered the eleven o'clock sermon in Otis Wheeler's shirt, at least a size too small for him. He hoped his coat hid how tight it was. He couldn't fasten the collar, so his tie, which he luckily hadn't worn in the baptistry because of his robe, held Otis's shirt closed at the top. Through the whole sermon he had the urge to pull on the tie, instead he gripped the lectern harder.

He did not stand by the door to shake hands after the service. He wanted no one to get a close look at his strange attire. So, he retreated to the dressing area to retrieve his sodden clothes immediately after the service. He picked up the bundle from the bench where he had left it. El planned to go out the side door of the sanctuary and through the back door of his office. He could stay there until everyone left. He turned to go and found himself face to face with the church treasurer, Leroy Boyd.

Leroy was not happy. His face had the color of an almost ripe tomato and his gray eyes held a nasty glint. "I want to talk to you, Preacher."

"Sure, Brother Leroy. Right now?" What was eating at the man? El had not seen that expression on Leroy's face before.

Leroy nodded. "Right now. I read that draft of the new church manual you sent me. It won't work."

"Well, it's still subject to revision, but the committee . . ."

"Hang the committee! You're the one behind it. I know that. You're trying to get rid of me. There's no church treasurer."

El understood now. Leroy had been church treasurer before El came to Hill Country Baptist Church. Now, he thought El had gone behind his back to get rid of him. El could set him straight on that. He needed Leroy's support for the new church manual. He had assumed he would have it. Leroy had never seemed interested in being a power broker in the church. He had always supported El.

"That's right, Leroy," El said. "But there is a finance committee. I was counting on you to head it."

Leroy took a step back. "Chairman of the finance committee? Would I still be in charge of counting the offering on Sunday, and the accounts?"

"If you want to be. The revision committee was just trying to lighten the load." *And break the stranglehold some old church members had on church affairs,* El added to himself. But Leroy had not been one of those. That's why his reaction caught El by surprise.

"I don't mind. Are there any hitches?" Leroy's eyes narrowed. He was still suspicious.

"No. Well, you will be limited to a three-year term, but then you can serve on any other committee you want."

Leroy's color had started to fade to a dull plum, now it brightened again. "That won't do. I like this job. I shouldn't be forced out of it."

El reached over and patted Leroy on the shoulder. "No one's forcing you out. Why don't we meet for lunch later this week and talk this out. We can both think about it some more. Maybe we can modify the manual." *If we do, all those others we are trying to phase out will want to be permanent too,* El thought.

Oh, Lord, what's the use? Trying to make changes in a Baptist church was like trying to dam a stream with sand, the water just went around and back into the original streambed. Eventually, the sand washed away, just as pastors were eventually worn away.

Leroy nodded slowly, but his color didn't change. "Okay. How 'bout lunch on Tuesday?"

El nodded. "Tuesday."

Leroy stalked off clutching a small blue bag in his left hand. The morning offering. Leroy would count it today, leave a note with the amount of the offering in the office, and deposit the offering tomorrow. *Maybe I am foolish, thought El.* Leroy does all that every Sunday, keeps the books for the church, and even locks up on Sunday so the janitor can leave by eleven-thirty. All for free. Still, new blood was healthy for a church. He would have to think of a way to placate Leroy without jeopardizing the other changes in the manual. He hoped it could be done. *Lord, I'll need your help on this one.*

El went out the side door. He stopped and glanced around. Only a few cars were still in the parking lot. The crowd had cleared out quickly. El headed for his car. No one appeared as he got in. El pitched his wet clothes in the backseat. In a car as old as his Mustang, you didn't need to worry about the upholstery.

It was a relief when he reached his small cabin not far from the church, just one bedroom, and a living area with the kitchen included, but big enough for him. El changed clothes. Shorts and T-shirt now. Since it was summer, there was no Sunday evening worship service. El hoped the congregation members used the time to be with their families. He planned to spend the rest of the day reading, but not some thought-provoking religious tome. El preferred science fiction. Briefly, he thought of his argument with Leroy. Was there someone on the church manual committee that could help him get around Leroy? El could not think of anyone. Well, he wouldn't let it spoil the rest of his Sunday. He would work on the problem of Leroy tomorrow.

▲2▼

MONDAY MORNING, EL tried to hurry as he strode up the loose-pebble walk in front of the church office. The river gravel scrunched beneath his shoes and slowed him down. For the thousandth time, he wondered when the church would find money to pave the walk. Not soon. Not as long as the current board of deacons was around. They hated to spend the church's money more than they hated to spend their own. El wiggled his shoulder blades; even with his coat off, sweat trickled down between them. Well, the radio had said it was eighty-seven already. What could you expect for August? El glanced at his watch. Nine o'clock. He'd promised his secretary, Martha, that he'd be in well before his nine o'clock appointment with Jack Nabors. And Nabors must be here already. There was a car parked next to the sanctuary. Why was it way over there when there was plenty of room by the office?

Why had he made this appointment on Monday morning? He never was much good after preaching twice on Sunday, and then there had been the baptisms. Those baptisms. The two girls had been all right, a little giggly, but ten-year-olds couldn't help that. But Tom Rivers, what a disaster. El giggled himself. *Sorry, Lord, but he did look just like Frankenstein's monster.*

"Why, Lord, did Tom slip, and we both end up under

water? Cause I thought of him as a monster?'' he asked. "Punishing me, Lord?'' El shook his head. "Starting early talking to you, Lord. I know it wasn't punishment.''

El pictured Tom Rivers the Sunday three weeks earlier when he came forward to join the church, a big, hulk of a man, ill-shaven with his shirttail hanging out. At least then, El hadn't thought of him as Frankenstein's monster. Tom, at the age of forty, had met Jesus and wanted to demonstrate his newfound faith by baptism. El admired any grown man who made that decision. He had shaken Tom's hand and congratulated him. Tom had looked at El and muttered. "I'm afraid of water.''

El had patted him on the back and said, "We'll talk later.'' Looking back now, El realized the jiggle in his stomach at Tom's words should have warned him of the impending disaster.

El shook his head as he climbed the wooden office steps two at a time. He hoped the week turned out better than yesterday. Even an argument with Brother Leroy. That could be a bad problem. He'd have that lunch with Leroy tomorrow, then decide how best to act. Maybe he would talk to Sister Alice; she always seemed to know how to handle people. El opened the door and walked into the reception area. The room was wonderfully cool. "Thank you, God, for air conditioning,'' El said under his breath.

Martha Wingate, the church secretary/receptionist, sat at her gray, metal desk in the center of the reception area sorting the mail. She wore an off-white dress that matched the walls and ceiling. Only a large navy blue bow at her throat kept her from seeming a fixture herself. Her desk was spotless, no loose papers or books. El envied Martha's ability to always keep the reception area neat. His office never looked like this. Even her typewriter, on a table to her left, was covered with its plastic cover since she was not using it.

She glanced up at him, then furtively at the clock.

"I know, Martha. I'm late."

"It's all right, Pastor. Mr. Nabors canceled his appointment."

"Really? Then whose car is that in the parking lot?"

Martha shook her head. "It was there when I got here. I figured someone left it yesterday."

El nodded. Church members occasionally left cars like that. Still, he usually was told. El remembered Nabors. "Did Mr. Nabors say why he couldn't make it?"

Before Martha could answer, El heard someone on the steps outside, someone in a hurry. El jumped away from the door just as it opened. Harry Jackson, the church custodian, stood in the doorway. He was as wet as El had been yesterday. His gray hair was plastered against his skull, and his clothes clung to his thin, bony body. A puddle formed at his feet as he spoke.

"Mr. El, Mr. El, you gotta come quick." His voice quivered with either excitement or fear.

Harry wasn't one to panic easily, El knew. Thirty years as a church custodian had been great training. For Harry to sound like that, disaster must have struck. A twinge of adrenaline-driven nausea made El gulp.

"I'm coming," he said, but Harry was already out the door, heading for the sanctuary across from the parking lot. El followed at a trot. Harry moved quickly for a man of seventy. El caught up with him at the side door of the sanctuary.

"It's bad, Mr. El. It's bad."

El asked no questions, for one thing he was too out of breath, and two, Harry obviously wanted him to see the cause of his anxiety. Harry never talked much anyway. Had the baptistry sprung a leak? That seemed to be where they were headed. A trail of puddles on the floor led that way. Just Harry's footprints, El decided.

The baptistry was inset into the stage so El could not see into it from the floor of the sanctuary. A good deal of water had been splashed onto the stage. Had someone fallen in?

El climbed the steps to the stage after Harry who seemed more agitated than ever. From the third step, he could see into the baptistry.

"Good Lord!" El exclaimed and almost stumbled on the next step.

Floating face down in the baptistry was a man in a suit. El recognized the man even in that position. Leroy. The water was a faint pinkish yellow. Blood? El started toward the baptistry steps, but Harry grabbed his arm.

"Don't, he's cold dead. I lifted him to see. Someone shot him in the chest."

El took a deep breath. *Calm yourself, be calm,* he told himself. "Harry, go back to the office. Tell Martha to call the sheriff. When he gets here, bring 'em over. I'll stay with the body."

Harry nodded and left, leaving a new set of puddles. El paced around the baptistry once, then stopped. He'd better not move around; he might disturb something that was evidence. Suddenly, he froze. The offering. Leroy had left him yesterday to count the offering in the vestibule between the men's and women's dressing rooms. El hurried back there.

There was the blue bank bag on the small table Leroy used for the counting. El picked it up and looked inside. It looked like the checks and money were there. He put the bag down. Better leave it alone until the sheriff arrived.

El made his way back to the stage. He stood beside the baptistry for a moment. He couldn't take his eyes off the body. He shuddered. Better wait down on floor level, then he wouldn't have to see Leroy. When he reached floor level El glanced around at the pews. Where had Leroy sat Sunday?

Good God! Leroy's family. The man had a wife and

two little kids. Damn! Would the sheriff tell them? He'd better try to be along.

He'd better call Wayne McCarty, his deacon chairman. What would he say? "Hi, this is your pastor. Just wanted to tell you I saw Leroy this morning, floating in the baptistry."

El suppressed a giggle. Get a hold of yourself. He did what he always did when he needed composure. He prayed.

"Dear Lord, forgive me for my failures. Please help me to bring comfort to those in need. Take care of Leroy."

He was still praying when the deputy arrived with Harry. El looked a second time. The deputy was a woman.

"Deputy sheriff Joyce Nelson. You're?" the woman said.

"El Littlejohn, I'm the pastor here at Hill Country."

The deputy frowned. She was a chunky woman, dressed in the standard deputy's outfit of tight-fitting, dark brown pants and shirt. The gun on her hip looked enormous.

"El?" she asked.

"Yes, E-l, short for Eldon. My full name is Eldon Lee Littlejohn. El is my nickname."

The deputy took a small notebook out of her pocket and wrote in it. "You're the pastor, right."

"Yes, I've been here two years."

"Age?"

"35"

"Address?"

"821 Driftwood."

"That the La Heredad subdivision?"

"Yes."

The deputy nodded and continued with her questions. Finally, she snapped her notebook closed.

"Show me the body," she ordered.

El nodded and led the way up the steps to the baptistry. He pointed although it wasn't necessary.

Deputy Nelson's brown eyes showed no hint of an expression as she looked in the baptistry. El wondered if she had seen many bodies in her career. She reopened her notebook.

"Know him?" she asked.

"Yes, his name is Leroy Boyd. He lives north of here, off Haynie Flat road."

"Full name?"

"I don't know. Wait." El remembered Leroy introducing himself. He always used his full name. "Leroy Woodrow Boyd." El nodded to himself in satisfaction. *I'm getting better at names, huh, God?*

"You find him?"

"No, Harry did." El nodded at Harry.

Joyce Nelson turned to Harry. She repeated her questions, which Harry dutifully answered until she had all the information she needed about him. Then she said, "Tell me how you found him."

Before Harry could answer, three men with a stretcher on wheels entered the sanctuary through the main doors and hurried toward them. Each was dressed in jeans, boots, and a white shirt with a tie tucked in below the second button of the shirt. *From the medical examiner,* El guessed. The deputy turned her attention to them.

"Up here. The body is in the baptistry. Get it out of the water, but wait for Lieutenant Coronado before you do anything else. He's on his way."

The men nodded as they climbed the steps to the stage. Once there, they spread a black body bag on the floor. One of them knelt and reached out to pull Leroy out of the water. The others knelt beside him to help. Without too much effort, they got Leroy's sodden body, face up, on the bag.

El looked at Leroy. He'd been a handsome man, almost too good-looking. Now his gray eyes stared sightlessly at the ceiling, and his brown hair, usually so carefully arranged, straggled across his face. Almost in the center of his chest was a small, dark hole. Someone was a good shot.

El said another prayer for Leroy's soul. Somehow, looking at his body, he was sure that Leroy needed it.

The deputy turned her attention back to Harry. "Okay."

Harry took a deep breath. "I came in to clean this mornin' and saw water on the floor."

"You clean here every Monday?"

"No, only after there's been a baptism."

The deputy looked at El.

"Yes, we had three baptisms yesterday."

"Him?"

"No, he's one of my deacons and the church treasurer."

She turned back to Harry. "Go on." She scribbled something in her notebook.

"When I saw him, I jumped in the baptistry. I thought he might still be alive, I guess. I lifted him up. He was cold and . . . I knew he was dead, so's I let him drop and went for the preacher."

El didn't hear the rest of the exchange between Harry and the deputy. More men came in, and El had to move to the back of the stage. Two more deputies in uniform and two men in suits. *Hot weather for suits,* El thought. One of the suited men spoke to one of the men in white shirts. The white-shirted man shooed everyone away from the body and squatted beside it. He said something to one of the deputies.

El couldn't hear what was said. One of the suited men turned and looked at El. There was a badge hanging from his pocket. He was a dark-complected, black-eyed, solid block of a man, a Mexican-American, El noted with surprise. There were not many minorities in the sheriff's department.

El soon found himself crowded into the men's dressing room behind the stage with Harry and the Mexican-American officer. He introduced himself as a homicide investigator, Lieutenant Coronado. Everything El had told the deputy had to be repeated for him. Just like the deputy's, Coronado's eyes never changed as Harry and El repeated the morning's events.

Deputy Nelson appeared at the door. "We found two sets of keys in Boyd's pocket. I tried the car keys on that car outside. Mr. Jackson said it was here when he arrived this morning. The keys fit."

Coronado held out his hand, and the deputy dropped the car keys into them. He turned them over in his hand, then handed them back to the deputy. Thanks."

He turned back to El, frowning. "That car sit in the parking lot all night?" he asked El.

"I guess so."

"Isn't that strange?"

"No, lots of people go places after church together and leave a vehicle here. They pick it up later, but sometimes not till the next day. We have no evening services in the summer. Leroy locks, I mean, locked up after Sunday morning services."

Coronado nodded, but seemed dissatisfied. "How come Mr. Boyd locked up, not your janitor?"

"Harry has another job on Sunday. He cleans for the Bible church about a mile from here. He likes to get there before their service lets out."

"I see," the lieutenant said.

Coronado asked El to count the money in the bank bag to see if it appeared to be the correct amount. El opened the bag. Alice Taylor's check was on top. El smiled. You could always count on Sister Alice. She had even helped with the baptisms yesterday. He finished as quickly as he could. The amount appeared close to the usual, not enough to meet the week's expenses. Hill Country always went in the hole in August.

He told Coronado, who nodded. "You can keep the offering, Reverend. I imagine your church needs it."

"Yes, I'll deposit it this afternoon."

Coronado insisted on going over everything again, so El did not get to go with the deputy that told Mrs. Boyd her husband was dead. El asked to go, but Lieutenant Coronado requested he stay. El knew that the request was a command. So it was almost noon before the church was empty, and Harry and El stood by the baptistry once more. El still had Sunday's offering, he hadn't even been able to get across the parking lot to the church office. Harry, however, had escaped for a while during the morning and had changed clothes.

"Better drain it, Harry. Wash it out good." He didn't want any future converts to be literally washed in blood. Lieutenant Coronado had taken a water sample and told El it was okay to clean the baptistry.

Harry nodded.

El left Harry and walked back to the office. The heat of the sun pressed in on him. He could feel the back of his neck getting red. He should wear a hat, he thought absently. *What next? Leroy's wife.* He had to go see Mrs. Boyd. He dreaded that.

The air-conditioned interior of the church-office building was an oasis of relief from the August heat. Martha was still at her desk.

"Can you call Wayne McCarthy and tell him about Leroy," El asked her. "Also, get hold of Steve Forbes, tell him what happened." Steve was the education/music minister for the church. Usually he came in on Mondays, but El hadn't seen him today.

Martha Wingate smiled her most motherly smile. El knew that she had long ago accepted the burden of looking after her unorganized pastor. "I've already told Steve. I left a message for Mr. McCarthy. He was out."

"Thanks, Martha."

El went to his desk. The church didn't have a safe,

but his desk did lock. He put the blue money bag in his file drawer, closed and locked it. The offering should be safe enough till he got back.

He stopped by Martha's desk on his way out. Martha smiled at him expectantly.

"I'm going to see Mrs. Boyd."

Martha's smile vanished and her face saddened. "You tell Sister Melanie, I'll be praying for her."

El nodded. "I'll tell her."

▲3▼

THE PEDERNALES RIVER was down, El noticed as he drove across the Highway 71 bridge fifteen minutes later. Even when spring rains were heavy like this year, Lake Travis dropped considerably by late in the summer. El turned his old Mustang onto Haynie Flat road a couple of miles past the bridge. The road was paved but twisting and narrow, and El had to drop his speed to thirty miles an hour. Five minutes later he pulled into the Boyd's driveway along side a brown and tan sheriff's car.

He took the cement walk to the house, wondering, as he had before, why Leroy had built a home here. It was over a mile to the nearest neighbor. He rang the door bell. Inside, the chimes played "The Eyes of Texas." Had Leroy gone to the University of Texas?

The marigolds growing next to the house rustled, but the wind against his face seemed more like an oven blast than a cooling breeze. Having his coat on didn't help; if someone didn't answer soon, he'd take it off.

Melanie Ann Boyd opened the door herself. Her red eyes and flushed skin contrasted with her crisply fresh, flowered dress. Even her hair was disheveled. Across her eyes hung a strand, which she kept pushing away. It reminded El of Leroy lying beside the baptistry. Obviously, the news of his death had hit her hard. El never remembered seeing her anything but perfectly made up.

"Mrs. Boyd, I've come to offer my condolences and to pray with you if you like," El said. He hadn't realized she was so short. She must be about five feet tall. He glanced at her feet. Sandals, of course. At church she wore heels.

"Oh, Pastor, I'm glad you came. Come in."

El followed her into the spacious living room. The furnishings spoke of wealth and good taste as well as comfort. El had only visited the Boyds a few times, usually to discuss church business with Leroy. Melanie sat down on the sofa. El joined her.

"Are you alone?"

Melanie nodded. "My mother's in Dallas. She's coming." Melanie blinked, fighting back tears. "There's a deputy going through Leroy's things. There were a bunch of officers here earlier. Now there's only one."

"I see. The children?"

"They're playing in the family room."

"Sister Melanie"—El switched to the more familiar—"would you like someone to stay with you until your mother gets here?"

"Pastor, I sure would, but I don't have many friends. I hardly know our neighbors."

"Don't you worry." El reached out and patted her hand. "I know someone who'll be glad to come. Just let me make a call."

In a minute, El had Alice Taylor on the phone. "Sister Alice, this is Brother El. I need a favor."

"Of course, Pastor. What?"

El smiled to himself. Alice was one of the handful at church he could always count on to help, not criticize. She must be in her late seventies, but you'd never know it.

"Leroy Boyd's been killed. Shot. His wife is all alone with the kids. Could you come over?"

"Oh, dear," Alice's voice shook a little. El realized

what a shock the news must be. He should have been less blunt.

"Sister Alice, you okay?"

"I'm fine. Where do the Boyds live?" Her voice had regained its strength.

Briefly, El gave directions. "Thanks, Sister Alice," he said. Her reply was barely audible. El returned the phone to its cradle.

He turned to Melanie. "Mrs. Taylor will be here soon. She has a ranch north of here. Do you remember her from church?"

"Yes, I do. Will you stay till she comes?"

"Of course."

Someone cleared their throat behind him. He turned to find himself looking into the rather cold eyes of Deputy Nelson.

"I'm through for now," she said looking at Melanie. "I may have to come back."

"Very well," Melanie said.

"I'll see you out," El said stepping forward. Melanie made no move to rise.

The deputy nodded.

She stopped at the door. "Do you know if Mr. Boyd had another source of income besides his construction business?"

El shook his head. Leroy had been a deacon and the church treasurer, but he and El had not had a warm relationship. Leroy never confided in El. "No, I never heard him say anything about his business. Maybe Melanie knows."

The deputy shook her head. "She's been questioned. Claims she knew nothing about her husband's business." She shrugged her shoulders. "Maybe."

She stared hard at El. "I'll be seeing you."

"Good-bye." El was unable to say anything else.

He waited with Melanie for Alice Taylor.

They talked about the weather, her children, but not about her husband.

"Would you like to pray with me about your loss?" El finally asked.

Melanie looked at him with haunted eyes. "I don't know if I should."

El was about to reassure her that no matter where Leroy got his money or the circumstances of his death, her loss was real and painful, when she continued.

"He treated me and the kids bad sometimes. I'm almost relieved he's dead."

El sat back. "Why didn't you say something? I always thought you two had a good marriage."

Melanie shook her head. "It was okay, except when he was drinking."

"Drinking?" El was astonished. He had heard Leroy rail against the evils of drink. Their church covenant specified total abstinence from alcohol as did those of most Southern Baptist churches. El was not naive enough to think that all his members held to that, but those who didn't usually made no secret of it, and they didn't speak out against drinking.

"Yes, but only once in a while. He got real mean when he drank."

El reached out and patted her hand again. "I'm sorry. I wish I had known. We can still pray."

"I'd like that." Melanie's eyes glistened with tears.

El bowed his head. "Dear Lord, Creator of all the world, Savior, we ask for your help in these trying times. Be with Sister Melanie and her children. Give them your strength in these dark days. Lead them into the light. Brother Leroy sinned, Lord, but we all fall short of your glory. Help us to remember that as we remember Leroy. We know that Leroy believed in you, Lord, whatever he did and that he is with you now. Again, be with his loved ones in this time of loss. I pray in your name, Jesus. Amen."

El looked at Melanie. What should he say to her now? Outside, a car crunched gravel as it approached. El stood up, relieved. "That must be Mrs. Taylor. I'll get the door."

The doorbell chimed. El opened the door. In front of him stood a petite, white-haired woman. Her brown eyes sparkled with an energy that belied her years.

"Sister Alice, thanks for coming. Mrs. Boyd really needs you."

Alice Taylor shut her eyes for a long moment; her color seemed to fade; her vivacity drained away. She was an old woman. El had never seen her look like that.

"Sister Alice, you okay?" He feared she was ill. If something happened to Alice Taylor, El could be in real trouble at Hill Country. She had been on the pulpit committee that had called him, and she had supported him ever since.

Alice Taylor opened her eyes and looked at El. "I'm fine. This just brings back memories of when I lost my James." She reached out and took his arm. "Introduce me, Brother El."

El finished the introductions quickly. Both women had seen each other at church, yet never really met. Alice Taylor took charge. She turned to El.

"You can run along now. I'll look after Melanie and the children."

El hesitated.

Alice Taylor frowned slightly.

El got the message. He said his good-byes and left.

He drove back to the church deep in thought. How little he knew of some of the people he served. The church was not too large, about two hundred men and women, not including children. Just about the perfect size in El's opinion. There were fewer children than in most churches of a similar size because many of the church members were past those years. This area was a haven for retirees who had fled the nearby city of Austin but wanted to stay close enough to still use its amenities. Some change had occurred two years ago when a new subdivision opened. Most of the younger families lived there. Their presence had breathed new life into the church.

El sometimes liked to think that it was his doing, the church growth, new programs, and younger people. But he knew that he had not been responsible, just lucky in his timing. The subdivision had opened just before he answered the call of Hill Country, and as it grew so had the church. The new people provided support he needed to make changes in the church. So far, they had remained loyal to him.

El remembered how glad he had been to leave behind that job as minister of education at the church in Austin. He had seriously been considering leaving the ministry until he got the call to Hill Country. He always wondered why they had called him. When he had visited Hill Country and given a sermon, the congregation's response had been friendly, but, he thought, not enthusiastic. Yet, Hill Country had called him. Maybe he should have quit the ministry instead of coming here. El shook his head. That was one of his problems, self-doubt. If only God could be more specific, show him definitely what to do.

"Lord, I want to be your servant. Show me your will," he said aloud. "Specific instructions would sure be helpful, Lord."

As usual he got no answer. The pavement changed as he drove across the Pedernales bridge, and the Mustang jumped a little. El chuckled to himself. If God answered now, he would probably drive off this bridge. He glanced downstream. People were skiing, even on a weekday. *Leroy liked to water ski,* El remembered.

Leroy and his family had been members before El had come to Hill Country. Leroy was considered a pillar of the church, always able to give a little extra money when the church was in need. El corrected himself, *had* been a pillar of the church. After a moments reflection, El changed his mind. Maybe not such a pillar. Leroy had not been active beyond his job as Treasurer. While he had been a deacon, he rarely attended the meetings. Only often enough to stay on the active roster. El had accepted him for what he saw, a reserved, hardworking man who loved his wife and kids. El shook his head again. That was one of his problems, seeing the outward person, never the inner. He just couldn't tell what was going on inside someone.

El was back where he was a few minutes before. *Should he have entered the ministry?* He had had a choice: graduate school or seminary. He had just received his Bachelor's degree in chemistry and been accepted for graduate school at Berkeley, when he had received God's call. El sighed. He believed in that call, what worried him was whether it had been to the ministry. He certainly had thought so at the time, only the years had dimmed the experience, and sometimes he felt ill-equipped to be a minister of Christ.

Resolutely, El turned his mind to planning the rest of the day. He had better not waste time with doubts. He needed to check to see if anyone was in the hospital, then deposit the offering and see what kind of state the church finances were in.

Before long, El turned his car into the church's drive, but his mind was once more struggling with his doubts. Maybe if he wasn't single . . . No, that would only complicate his life, and his income really wouldn't support another.

Suddenly, he realized that the parking lot was full of cars and vans. His heartbeat quickened when he saw that at least two were from the local TV stations. He parked his car and headed for the church office.

Martha greeted him with a strained smile. "I was just

going to call you, Pastor. Mr. Gunter is in your office, and there are reporters in the church. Steve is showing them the baptistry.''

El nodded and headed for his office. Best to get the worst over with first. Bill Gunter, a deacon and one of the church's trustees, paced El's office. His back was to El as he entered. Unfortunately for El, Bill Gunter always made him think of a department store dummy, somewhat unreal except for his shiny, bald head. El wondered why a man as vain as Bill didn't wear a toupee. Maybe, he knew that the thin fringe of brown hair he still had made him less imposing. Bill Gunter turned. He was impeccably dressed as usual in a gray suit, white shirt and tie, even his shoes were gray.

''There you are. It's about time,'' Gunter said.

El caught the edge of anger in his voice. ''I've been with Mrs. Boyd. Got someone to stay with her.'' Bill Gunter was a real power in the church, he'd helped to start it, and now as a trustee he represented the church in all business deals. El had to handle Brother Bill carefully.

Bill frowned. ''Well, you could have sent Forbes.''

El only nodded. He didn't want to get Steve in trouble by telling Bill he had not been here this morning. Steve was a hard worker. When he took time off it was deserved. Besides, even if Steve had been at the office, El would still have gone.

''This is bad business,'' Bill continued. ''Look at all the press out there. Bad.''

''I didn't think about the press getting hold of this,'' El admitted.

Bill stepped closer to him. ''You should have. You should have thought of the church first. Before you took off. And why didn't you notify me immediately?''

''Maybe you're right, Brother Bill. Things just happened so fast. All I could think of was Mrs. Boyd and those kids of hers, alone. Sister Alice is staying with

her.'' El deliberately played his biggest card when he
mentioned Alice Taylor. Like Bill Gunter, Alice Taylor
and her husband had been founders of this church, and
as far as El could tell, Alice Taylor was the only one
that Bill Gunter respected at Hill Country and the only
one with as much clout. But because she was a woman,
she could not be a deacon or a trustee.

Bill grunted, ''Good. Sister Alice knows what she's
doing.''

El relaxed until Bill continued.

''You should have called her to go, and you should
have stayed here. Why didn't you call me?''

El swallowed and told the man the truth. ''I just didn't
think to tell you.''

Bill Gunter scowled at El. ''Don't ever do that again,
Pastor.''

Pastor came out with a heavy overtone of malice. El
knew what was unsaid. Toe the mark that Bill Gunter
drew or lose this church. The worst was that Bill Gunter
could do it. Even with the support of the new people in
the church, if Bill Gunter wanted him gone, El doubted
he could hang on.

''I'm sorry, Brother Bill. It won't happen again.'' El
wanted to ask, how the heck he found out, but thought
he better not. To his surprise Bill supplied the information.

''It was lucky my friend at the TV station called me.
Otherwise, I wouldn't have known still. Now I want you
to get out there with that press and handle 'em. Make it
plain that the church is not involved. That it's just a
coincidence that Leroy got shot here.''

''I'll try,'' El said. He wasn't sure how to keep the
church out of it when the murder victim had been found
floating in the baptistry.

He left his office quickly. The media were bound to
be easier to handle than Bill Gunter. Martha smiled apol-
ogetically. She probably felt guilty for not thinking to

call Gunter. El tried to smile reassuringly at her, but she didn't look like it helped. El would have to soothe her later. Now, he needed to be in that sanctuary.

He decided to enter by the main doors at the back of the sanctuary, that way he could see what was going on down front without being immediately noticed. A minute later, El opened one of the doors and slipped into the rear of the sanctuary. Steve Forbes was standing at the edge of the baptistry while the press people congregated at his feet in front of the stage. Steve saw El.

"Here's the man you need to speak to, our pastor, Eldon Littlejohn." The relief in Steve's voice was clear.

The group of men and women in front of Steve seemed to turn in unison toward El.

"Good afternoon. How can I help you?" El said as he walked forward. Could he think of anything more inane to say?

The next few minutes were a barrage of questions. Most just concerned the discovery of the body. Harry had disappeared it seemed, so El was the only one available to describe the scene this morning. Then the questions turned more personal.

A female reporter from one of the TV stations asked, "Do you know why Mr. Boyd was here alone?"

"Mr. Boyd was our church treasurer. He counted the money after church, but the money was still here this morning."

"What other reasons would anyone have for killing Boyd? Was he having an affair? Maybe a jealous rival?"

El put on his sternest expression. "Leroy Boyd was a deacon of this church. He was not the kind of man to have an affair. I think such questions are out of line."

The reporter shrugged her shoulders.

A few more questions followed, then the TV crews requested that El stand beside the baptistry while they took pictures. El reluctantly took his place. He glanced down. Harry had wasted no time, the baptistry was dry.

Thank God. At least there would be no pictures of blood-stained water.

Finished, the reporters drifted away. All, however, said they would be in touch. El hoped he never saw them again. He headed back to his office.

Bill Gunter was gone. El dropped into his chair and closed his eyes.

"Dear Lord, I need strength. I love these people. Don't let this murder hurt them. For all my self-doubts, I don't want to leave this church. Please, God, show me what to do."

▲4▼

LUCKILY, NO ONE from church was in the hospital this week. El could put off his one nursing-home visit till later in the week. He wanted to get the church's money in the bank.

El retrieved the money bag from his desk. He sat down and counted the offering, and endorsed the checks. He and Leroy were the only ones that could do that. He'd have to get someone added. There was no deposit slip in the bag, not even a blank one. Leroy must have been killed before he counted the offering. El would have to get a deposit slip at the bank, Leroy had all the church's. El sighed. If he had been thinking, he could have retrieved all the church's stuff when he had been out at Leroy's home.

He told Martha where he was going, then left. The church used a downtown Austin bank. El had only been there once. That had been when he became pastor and signed a new signature card along with Leroy. When El first came to Hill Country, he wondered why the church used a bank so far away when there were several banks closer and more part of Hill Country's community. Leroy had told him that this bank gave them the best interest. El had not questioned him further.

The drive into town took him over half an hour. At least, the bank had a parking garage. He could have deposited the money at a drive-in teller, but he figured he better talk to a bank officer about Leroy's death.

He went to the reception desk and explained his errand. The young woman smiled and told him she would get someone to help him. A few minutes later, El was sinking into a rather plush arm chair in a vice-president's office. The vice-president had appeared almost immediately, a young man in an immaculate, dark blue suit, white shirt, and red tie. El was surprised that the man was so concerned about a small account like the church's. He introduced himself as Tom Penwell.

"Now, Reverend Littlejohn, did I understand that Mr. Boyd has died?"

"Yes," El said. He had better tell the man the truth. "Mr. Boyd was found this morning at our church. It appears he was murdered."

Penwell blinked. "Murdered. Was it theft?"

"No, the offering appears to be intact. That's what I came to do, to deposit it." El handed the blue bag to Penwell.

"I see."

"There's no deposit slip. I wrote down the total. Leroy, that is, Mr. Boyd, did all our bookkeeping and had all our supplies."

Tom Penwell nodded. "I'll take care of it. If you just wait here."

El waited.

The banker returned with a puzzled expression. "You said there had been no robbery?"

"That's right. That looked like about the right amount."

"Reverend Littlejohn, I did a quick computer check on your church's account. Have you seen one lately?"

El shook his head. "Mr. Boyd handled that. He sent the monthly statement to the church, though. I just haven't seen it lately. What's the problem?"

"This offering is way below what Mr. Boyd usually deposits."

"How far below?" El's heartbeat picked up. *Something was wrong here. What?*

"About fifty thousand dollars low."

El stared at Penwell. Fifty thousand dollars. That was more than ten times what they got on a good Sunday.

"There must be a mistake." El said. "Hill Country doesn't take in that much."

"No mistake, sir. Look." Penwell extended a computer printout.

El took it. It was a list of monthly deposits since the beginning of the year. Huge sums of cash were deposited every week.

"How much do we have in our account now?" El asked.

"Just a minute," Penwell said. This time he turned to the computer terminal on his desk. He punched some keys.

"About two hundred thousand. It appears that at the end of every month your church transfers most of the cash deposits to a foundation, the Woodrow Foundation."

El shook his head. "I've never heard of it. Why didn't our bank statements show this?"

Tom Penwell frowned. "They did, sir."

El shook his head. "Not the ones I saw. Could you get me a copy of the last two months?"

"Certainly," said Penwell. He got up and left.

El could not believe what he had just heard. If Penwell was telling the truth, then Leroy must have been supplying the church with bogus statements. El doubted the bank had any reason to lie. *What had been Leroy's game?* El suddenly felt a little sick to his stomach. *Money laundering. What a perfect scheme. Dear Lord, using the church for such evil.*

Penwell returned with the statements. "Here you go."

Just as he said, they showed large deposits of cash each week and a withdrawal at the end of the month.

"Thank you," El said. "I'll talk with my trustees and see if we can figure this out."

On the way back to church, El wondered what was going on. *Where had all that money come from? Where was it going?*

When he reached the office, he called the sheriff's department. Coronado was not in. El left a message for him to call.

He called Steve in next and filled him in on what El had learned at the bank. Steve's eyes grew round when El told him how much money was involved.

"What are you going to do?" Steve asked.

"Well, I'll tell the trustees and Brother Wayne tomorrow. Don't say anything to Martha yet. The money is not ours. Maybe the sheriff can figure out who it belongs to."

Steve nodded. They talked a few minutes more about the day's happenings, then Steve went back to his office.

A little before five, Harry came by to say he was leaving. El remembered with amusement how miraculously he'd appeared after the reporters left.

"I scrubbed out the baptistry with disinfectant, and rinsed it out good. I'll fill it tomorrow," Harry said.

El nodded.

Harry gave a half wave and left.

The rest of the staff gradually trickled away. At half past five, El was ready to go out the door when the phone rang. It was Wayne McCarty, the chairman of deacons at Hill Country.

"I just got the message, Pastor. I can't believe it. Leroy dead. And in the baptistry."

"Yes, it's a shock. I visited Mrs. Boyd. She was all alone, so I got Alice Taylor to stay with her." El wondered if Wayne had talked to Bill Gunter. Wayne and

El got along pretty well, but Wayne would jump to whichever way Bill said.

"Good. What Sunday School class is she in, Pastor?"

"I don't know." El closed his eyes. He had never even thought to check.

"Pastor, you should have found out and called the teacher."

"Yes, you're right, Brother Wayne." To himself El said, *You are right, Wayne, but why do you have to point out my failings like that.* He continued aloud. "I'll have Martha take care of it in the morning."

"You do that, Pastor. Some of the deacons will go visit Mrs. Boyd tomorrow. See if she needs anything."

"That'll be good, Brother Wayne." El hesitated, but he better tell Wayne about the money. "Brother Wayne, do you know anything about large cash deposits by this church?"

"How large?" Wayne asked.

Briefly, El explained. When he finished he waited for a reply.

There was a short silence, then Wayne said, "Pastor, that sure sounds like Brother Leroy was doing something illegal. Would you mind if I checked with Brother Bill about this?"

"Not at all," El answered, relieved he didn't have to deal with Gunter. He had been dreading telling him.

"Boy, I just wonder what Leroy was up to," Wayne said. "He could be darn shut-mouthed."

"Brother Leroy is dead. I think it best we just focus on the living now."

"You're right, Pastor. Talk to you later. Bye."

"Good-bye, Brother Wayne." El smiled to himself; that he was right about anything was a real concession from Wayne McCarty.

El wasted no time leaving the office. He didn't want to be caught by another late call. Once outside, he did stop to look at the church building. It was a spreading, unpretentious structure of limestone, housing the sanctuary, fellowship hall, and education facilities. El frowned. One of the main sanctuary doors was ajar. He'd have to speak to Harry tomorrow. Although it probably wasn't his fault, someone else had most likely left it open, it was Harry's responsibility to see the doors were locked at night and unlocked in the morning, except on Sundays. On Sundays, Leroy locked up.

Had the church been locked when Harry arrived this morning? He'd have to ask Harry. That sheriff's lieutenant probably had asked.

El frowned. Coronado had not returned his call. Well, tomorrow would be soon enough to tell him about the money.

As El walked toward the open sanctuary door, he remembered how thrilled he had been to be called to this church. Sometimes it was hard for him to recall that feeling of elation.

El grabbed the doorknob to pull the door shut. *Did something move inside?* He opened the door wide and stepped into the sanctuary. His Mustang was the only car left in the parking lot, even Leroy's had been taken away. Everyone was gone. El hoped some animal hadn't gotten in. All he needed was a skunk wandering through the pews. He didn't switch on the lights. The sanctuary had a skylight that provided plenty of illumination.

"Harry?" he shouted. Maybe Harry had forgotten something and left his truck on the road instead of driving back in. That way he wouldn't have to turn his old pickup around, sometimes it didn't like to reverse.

There was no answer.

El walked down the wide center aisle of the church, glancing left and right down each row of padded wooden pews. There was no sign of any furry beast. He reached the front of the church, moved to the right and climbed the steps to the stage. He walked to the rear past the empty baptistry. It was still uncovered. Harry must have wanted to be sure it dried out.

El thought he heard something. Was there someone in the dressing rooms?

He called. "Anyone there?" He didn't think an animal would come up here.

No answer.

He hesitated, then slipped into the entryway behind the stage. To his left was the men's dressing area, to his right the women's. Directly in front of El was the little, wooden table on which Leroy counted the morning offering. Behind it was a linen closet. The closet doors gaped open, and most of the towels and baptismal robes were dumped on the floor.

"Damn," said El under his breath.

He stepped past the fallen linens and headed for the men's side. It was empty. He retraced his steps to the linen closet. He was about to examine the ladies' side when he heard a noise on the stage. El swung round. He'd find out who was fooling around. Probably a kid or worse, a reporter.

El stopped at the edge of the empty baptistry to scan the sanctuary. Someone could hide behind the pews or in the choir loft above and behind him. El started to turn to check. Without warning someone leaped toward him from behind the pulpit. El caught a glimpse of an upraised arm. He flung his left arm up to ward off the attack and stepped back into nothingness. His arms flailed as he fought to keep his balance. He expected a blow at any moment. Before his assailant could reach him, El's other foot slipped, and he toppled into the empty baptistry.

The metal structure clanged when El's back hit the bottom. The sound filled his head. Stunned, El lay still. Was he hurt? He couldn't move. All he could do was gasp for air. He waited for his attacker to leap upon him. Instead, he heard the sound of someone running, then the sanctuary door groaned as it was opened too quickly. El closed his eyes.

When he opened them again, he realized he didn't know how long it had been. Had he passed out? He could see the roof above clearly. At least, it was still light.

Carefully, he stood up, relieved that there did not seem to be any great damage. He winced as he started up the baptistry steps. His left knee felt as if someone was sticking an ice pick into it. Favoring that knee, he climbed out and staggered toward the sanctuary door, which was still ajar. He held on to the doorknob for a moment as a wave of nausea washed through him, then he slowly closed and locked the door. It seemed to help to move slowly.

He limped toward his car trying to decide if a trip to the minor emergency clinic was warranted. Before he reached it, he heard the crunch of gravel as a car swung into the church drive. As he turned to see who was driving, El wondered if his attacker had returned. His heartbeat quickened. The setting sun made him squint. He held up an arm to block the light.

He still couldn't recognize the car, just a dark silhouette in the fading light. The car stopped.

"Reverend, what's wrong?"

El didn't recognize the voice, a woman's voice. "I fell in the baptistry."

"You're not wet."

El vaguely remembered the voice. Then he recognized the stocky form getting out of the car.

"It was empty, Deputy."

"You don't look too good." Deputy Sheriff Nelson stepped closer. She gripped his arm and steered him toward her car. El did not resist. The world seemed curiously distant. The deputy put him in the front passenger seat, then went to the other side and reached for her radio.

"I'm going to have EMS out here to look you over."

El didn't need an ambulance. He shook his head to stop the deputy, but the dull ache at the back of his head suddenly became a hot jab of fiery pain. He gingerly touched the back of his head and then stared in surprise at his bloody fingers. He hadn't known that he had hit his head.

Deputy Nelson shook her own head. "Dispatch, I need an ambulance at the Hill Country Baptist Church on Highway 71. The pastor has had an accident."

The dispatcher acknowledged. "EMS notified. They'll be there in six or seven minutes."

"What happened, Reverend?" Nelson asked. She'd come back around to his side of the car. She looked worried. *Why?*

"Someone was in the sanctuary. No. In the dressing area behind the baptistry. Left the sanctuary door open. I went to investigate and . . ." He wasn't doing a very good job of explaining what had happened. He had an overpowering urge just to shut his eyes and go to sleep.

Deputy Nelson leaned toward him. "Did you see who it was?"

"No, when I came out of the dressing area, someone tried to hit me, I think. I lost my balance and fell in the baptistry. Normally, it would be covered, you know." El stopped. Why had he added that last?

"Sure, Reverend. I understand. Just a bad day for the baptistry."

El was not sure he liked that last comment, but he decided to ignore it. "Don't call me reverend. Makes me feel old. Call me El."

"All right, El. You can call me Joyce. You sit here. I'm just going to walk around out here for a moment."

El watched the deputy walk toward the sanctuary. He closed his eyes.

"El, is the sanctuary locked now?"

The words brought him back from wherever he had

been. El opened his eyes and started to nod. He stopped. There was no pain now, but why take a chance.

"Yes," he said. He reached in his pocket and pulled out a key chain with several keys. "Here, these are to all the buildings. Search if you want to."

"Thanks, Reverend. Sorry. El."

Before the deputy could move, an ambulance turned into the drive, its siren wailing. El didn't remember them being so loud. The deputy waved to the driver. He pulled in on El's side of the deputy's car. In a moment, a paramedic was examining him. Another young man soon joined him.

"I think we better get him to Brackenridge. Can't tell about head wounds, and that knee of his is really swollen." The other paramedic nodded and picked up the receiver on their portable radio. He notified their dispatcher.

El listened. He felt very detached from his surroundings. If he could just go home and lie down. He opened his mouth to tell them, then decided it wasn't worth the effort. The first paramedic turned back to El. "We're going to take you to Brackenridge, okay?"

"Okay," El heard himself say, more of an echo than an agreement. He watched as the two men brought out a stretcher. He contemplated a protest again, but somehow . . .

Pain lanced up his leg all the way to his hip as they placed him on the stretcher. Momentarily, he was alert. "That hurt," he grunted.

"I know, sir. But I don't want to give you anything for pain until a doctor has looked at your head. Do you have a private physician we can notify?"

"No, haven't needed one."

"Okay. Don't worry, the doctors at the hospital are first class."

"See you later, El." Deputy Nelson leaned over the stretcher. "I'm going to take a look inside."

As the paramedic closed the ambulance doors, El saw the deputy toss the keys in the air and catch them.

El's head had cleared by the time the ambulance reached the emergency room at Brackenridge, the Austin-owned hospital. He told the paramedics, but they only nodded and smiled. A few minutes later, a young doctor was asking him questions and poking him in odd places.

"Your head wound looks superficial, but we'll get an X-ray anyway. I'm more concerned with that knee. Have you had problems with it before?"

El almost laughed. *Had trouble?* That knee was an endless source of torment. "Yeah, I tore it when I was a kid, playing touch football. It has never been the same."

"You should see an orthopedist; I can call one in."

"No, I've had their opinions before. Unless something is really messed up, can't you handle it?"

"I'll see, but I may have to call one in anyway."

El nodded. He expected he would see an orthopedist before this was over.

Two hours later, after X-rays of both his head and his knee and an examination by the orthopedist, El called Steve Forbes to come take him home. He almost called his parents who lived in northwest Austin, but he remembered that his father was out of town. No use alarming his mother. Besides, she'd make him go home with her. Steve was there a half hour later.

"You should have called as soon as you got here." Steve looked at him reproachfully.

"We spend enough time sitting around these hospitals. You needed to be home. Now see if you can spring me from this place."

Fifteen minutes later an orderly wheeled El to the door and helped him into Steve's car.

"Linda would be glad for you to stay with us for a

few days," Steve said as El settled into the seat and
fastened his seat belt.

"Linda has her hands full with you and the kids. Just
take me home."

Steve fussed the whole way to El's house. El had
purchased the house himself rather than have the church
furnish a parsonage. It was more a cabin than a house,
but it suited El. Tonight, El realized it had one draw-
back. It had lots of steps. The cabin was built on concrete pilings that raised it about nine feet off the ground
leaving room for a storage area and El's car. El loved
the view from the front deck, but now those steps to that
deck looked formidable.

Steve must have reached the same conclusion. "My
house doesn't have these steps," he said.

"I can make it if I take my time," El assured him.
He hoped that was true.

El started up with Steve beside him. He took the steps
one at a time, always careful not to bend his bad knee.
At last they made it to the top. El gave Steve his house
key and let him open the door.

Once inside El collapsed on the sofa. He was really
tired.

"You go now. I'll be all right," he told Steve.

Steve shook his head. "No I'll stay until you're in
bed." He was true to his word. He refused to leave until
he saw El settled in bed and they said a prayer together.

El realized with a shock that since he had been attacked not once had he thought of God. As soon as Steve
left, El apologized to God.

"I'm sorry Lord, I just got too wrapped up in myself.
I hope you understand. Amen."

▲5▼

TUESDAY MORNING, THE phone beside his bed woke El. He brought the receiver to his ear without sitting up. It was Lieutenant Coronado.

"How you doing? Reverend," he said.

"Fine," El said as he blinked at the clock. Nine o'clock. He had slept late. He sat up and remembered all of yesterday's events, especially the last ones. His knee throbbed, and his head ached dully. He hadn't felt this bad in years.

"You sure," Coronado said.

El chuckled. "No, I just sat up and I feel rotten."

"Oh, I woke you. I'm sorry." Coronado sounded genuinely sorry.

"That's all right. I needed to be up." El had a thought. "Did you catch the guy who hit me?"

"Sorry, not a trace, but we are still looking. No, I'm calling for a couple of reasons. First off, you left a message you wanted to talk to me."

El remembered. Briefly, he explained his visit to the bank and the results.

"You had no idea that kind of money was going through the church?"

"None at all. I was going to check with my trustees today, but I don't think I'll make it to the office. I'll talk to them on Wednesday unless you think it needs to be done today.''

"No, we'll check around. That's all I need right now. You take care.''

After El put the receiver back in its cradle, he remembered that Coronado had said he had a couple of things to discuss, but they had talked about only one. Well, he could talk to him tomorrow. He scooted back down in bed. He'd just relax a few minutes more. He fell asleep.

The phone woke him. It was Martha. Steve had told her what happened last night.

"I'm all right, Martha, but I don't think I'll come in today. Cancel my appointments, reschedule them if you can, but not for Wednesday." El paused, then went on. "Just tell people I took the day off, no use scaring them. But you better tell Bill Gunter and Wayne McCarty about last night. Tell them to call me if they want to.''

El got up and dressed. His head wasn't bad, but if he moved his knee the wrong way pain shot through it. He checked the freezer. There was a frozen breakfast of pancakes and sausage. He put it in the microwave and soon was enjoying a hot meal. After he finished, he knew he had another call to make. One he dreaded. His mother.

"Hi, Mom," he said when she answered.

"What's wrong?" she said.

"Now, Mother, why do you think something's wrong just because I called you.''

He heard her sigh. "Eldon Lee, you don't call me on weekday mornings. I saw the news. Is it about the church?''

"Sort of," El said, then he explained briefly.

"I'm coming right over. You should have come home last night, not stayed alone. Eldon Lee, what am I going to do with you?''

"Don't come, Mom. You're twenty miles away.''

"I'll be there in an hour," his mother said and hung up.

El put the receiver down. He should have known.

The phone rang. It was Steve checking on him. El assured him he was okay. Steve had nothing new to tell him. Almost as soon as he put the receiver down, the phone rang again. It was one of his church members who had just heard El had been hurt. El wondered who had told. Maybe it was just as well.

By the time his mother arrived, he was glad to see her. He hadn't been able to do anything but answer the phone as different church members and friends called to check on him. El had to admit that he had appreciated the attention. Maybe he wasn't such a bad pastor after all.

His mother cooked lunch for him. She had brought her own groceries to do so. She pointed this out to El as she surveyed his refrigerator. After lunch, El had called Melanie Boyd to check on the details of Leroy's funeral. It was scheduled for Friday. She had heard about his injuries. He assured her he was well able to perform the service.

Blanche Wheeler called next. El was surprised because she had called earlier. This time she wanted to speak to his mother. El felt like a boy again, being taken care of by the adults. He couldn't tell what the conversation was about from his mother's side of it.

His mother turned to him after she put the receiver down. "Mrs. Wheeler is coming over later. She will fix you supper. I'll go after she comes."

His mother was true to her word. She'd gone home after Blanche Wheeler arrived. Otis and Harry had brought his car to him. Blanche Wheeler had left after feeding him and cleaning the dishes. Once he was alone, El contemplated the day. All in all, it had been good. Knowing so many people were concerned about him was gratifying.

Wednesday morning, El's knee was almost pain free as he made breakfast. Thanks to his mother he had bacon and eggs. He switched on the TV for the news. Yesterday's paper had put Leroy's murder on the front page. The story mentioned a police investigation into Leroy's business activities. Hill Country Baptist Church had been mentioned more than once. Now, El wondered if the murder was still in the news. The local newscaster reminded him that the legislature was meeting in town. He remembered, a special session. The announcer's face was replaced by another's.

"I am calling on the governor to allow my bill to be introduced in this special session. Texas must take a stand against drugs. My bill will put all drug dealers and users on notice that Texas is not the place for them."

El quit listening. He had seen this guy before, Senator Marcus Matthew Depew from Dallas. He was always proposing the harshest penalties for some crime. El found his simplistic views distasteful. Worse though for El, Depew was a power in Baptist circles. He belonged to an ultra-conservative church in Dallas and through it had been appointed to several boards. He was always calling for a purge of the liberal elements of the Southern Baptist Convention. El had the uncomfortable feeling that anyone who did not agree with Marcus Matthew Depew was liberal.

El caught his last line: "I propose that anyone caught buying drugs should face a mandatory prison sentence of ten years for the first offense and anyone caught twice should be sent to jail for life."

The announcer's face reappeared. "It does not appear likely that the governor will open the special session to Depew's bill."

"Thank God," El said aloud. At least, the governor had some sense.

He finished breakfast and dressed for work. El knew from past experience that he better get in today. More than a day away from the office created chaos.

Martha greeted him with a warm smile as he entered the office. "Oh, Pastor, do you think you should work today?"

"I'm fine, Martha. Thanks. Just a little sore. Has anyone from the sheriff's office been around?"

"Not since, yesterday. They spent the whole morning in the church." Martha frowned.

"It's okay. I knew they'd be around."

El settled himself at his desk with a sigh. In the middle of it were his keys and a sheet of notebook paper. He picked up the paper. It was a thanks from Deputy Nelson. The printout from the bank was still on his desk, too. He wondered if all the trustees knew about it. He would have to check later. El had assumed since Wayne knew he would tell everybody else.

He looked at the pile of letters and papers in his IN box. Too bad that stuff couldn't be ignored. He straightened his leg. His knee ached now. Well, maybe work would take his mind off it. He reached for the stack of papers in his box. There was a knock on his door.

"Come in."

Harry shuffled in. His lined face seemed more deeply creased than usual.

"Good morning, Mister El. You doing okay?"

"I'm fine, Harry."

Harry glanced around the room, then looked hard at the floor.

"What's the matter, Harry?"

"Those deputies were asking a lot of questions yesterday."

"That's their job."

"'Bout you, sir."

"Oh." El took a quick breath. He should have realized that everyone was a suspect. He resisted the temptation to find out what they had asked Harry.

"Don't worry about me, Harry." El hoped his voice did not give him away.

"Well, they shouldn't bother with a preacher."

El nodded, but he thought of recent news stories. Ministers had been accused and sometimes convicted of all sorts of crimes including murder. The deputies had a reason to be suspicious.

Harry was fishing through his overall pockets now, muttering to himself. El tried not to smile. Harry picked up any nail, screw, washer, or other bit of hardware he saw lying around and stashed it in a pocket for possible future use. There was no way to know what odd bit of metal was the object of his search. El had seen him pull the most improbable objects out of one of those cloth repositories. Finally, Harry grinned and pulled a hairpin from his left front pocket.

"I found this in the baptistry when I cleaned it Monday. I was going to give it to the sheriff, but I forgot. They asked too many dadburned questions."

El couldn't keep from smiling now. Harry never used a bad word, but his "by" words as he called them meant the same. "Dadburn" was his favorite.

"Let me see it." El held out his hand.

Harry dropped the pin into it.

El looked at it. It was an ordinary hairpin that women used to hold long hair in place. El shrugged.

"I don't think it means much, Harry. You can give it to the sheriff if you want. Or I can."

Harry smiled, showing yellowed teeth. "You do that. I'd 'preciate it."

El nodded and dropped the hairpin in his paper clip holder. "Did you get the baptistry filled?"

"Yes, sir. And I put the cover back on." Harry looked at the floor again. "If I'd done that the other night, you wouldn't have been hurt. But I figured no one would be around. I wanted it to dry good, so I could make sure it was clean. I'm sorry."

"Harry, that open baptistry may have saved my life. If I hadn't fallen in, the guy that was after me might have gotten me."

Harry grinned again. "Oh, I hadn't thought of that. Thanks, Mr. El. I reckon I'll get back to work."

El nodded.

After Harry left, El fished out the hairpin. He played with it as he went over the events of Monday night. He had been very lucky, but as someone else once said, luck was just another name for God. El studied the hairpin he was fiddling with. It was sturdier than he expected. Probably one of the girls baptized Sunday dropped it. El stuck it back in the paper clip holder. His mind drifted back to Sunday. *Who had seen Leroy last?*

Steve Forbes interrupted his reverie. "El, you busy?"

El shook his head.

Steve plumped himself down in the chair next to El's desk. Steve had called him twice yesterday, but refrained from talking much church business. "Just want to bring you up-to-date."

The next few minutes were spent on mundane church matters. Then Steve said, "The trustees know about the money. Bill Gunter called them himself. No one knows where it came from. That deputy sheriff, Coronado, he talked to Brother Bill about the money, too. Maybe the other trustees, I don't know."

"I'm not surprised," El said. "That is a lot of money. Anything going on besides the stuff connected with Leroy?"

"Bea Cummings has it in her head that we're not doing enough mission work," Steve said with a frown. "She wants to talk to you about it."

El nodded. Bea Cummings chaired the Missions Committee and was the perennial president of the church's Women's Missionary Union. "I talked to her last week. She thinks our outreach program doesn't rate a missions label. She wants that money given either to the Cooperative Program or another Southern Baptist mission program. She also thinks we should support the Austin Baptist Association more.'' El knew that Bea would work on her husband to see that the deacons saw it her way.

Steve sighed. ''Why don't people see all the un-churched around them. We've got to get them. So many unsaved.''

El nodded again. He had managed to deflect Bea last year with the mission committee, but it looked like that wouldn't work this year. ''Well, I'll talk to her and try to placate her, but she may mess up the budget for next year if we don't keep on top of it.''

Now it was Steve's turn to nod in agreement.

''You going to handle prayer meeting tonight?'' Steve asked.

''Yes, I'll do it. At least, it's not a business meeting.''

Steve laughed. ''Thank God for small blessings.''

After Steve left, El started on his lesson for tonight. The phone rang. It was his mother. He was not surprised that she was checking on him today.

''Eldon Lee, don't hide anything from me.''

''I'm just fine, mother.'' When she used both his given names he knew she wanted his full attention.

''I called your house first. I didn't think you would go to work today.''

''Mom, I told you I planned to. There's Wednesday night supper, and I have to make a start on my sermon for Sunday.''

''Don't overdo.''

''I won't. How's Dad?'' El's father was still in California at a business meeting.

''He's fine. I told him about your accident when he called last night. He'll come home if you need him.''

''I'm okay. Don't let him cut his trip short.''

''Well, maybe you should stay with me until he gets back,'' his mother said.

"Thanks, Mom, but I'll stay at my place." This was a repeat of yesterday's conversation.

El heard his mother sigh. He was an only child, and he knew his mother didn't think she saw him often enough. "You take care," she said.

"Okay."

"I love."

"I love."

▲6▼

THE DAY PASSED surprisingly fast. Church members called to check on him. Alice Taylor was among them. She had only learned today of his accident. She seemed more reserved than usual. El hoped he had been right in asking her help with Melanie Boyd. He assured her as he had the others that he was fine. He had no visits or counseling scheduled because he always kept Wednesday clear so he had time to prepare for the evening's service. El half-expected a visit from the sheriff, but none came. He left the office at three, since he had to be back at five-thirty for supper and prayer meeting.

At five-thirty, he was in line in Fellowship Hall which doubled as the church cafeteria on Wednesday nights. It came as no surprise that the main course was barbecued chicken. El suspected that half the Baptist churches in Texas were having barbecued chicken tonight. El filled his plate and headed for a table. Soon, Steve Forbes and his family joined him, then Wayne McCarty and his wife, Kathy, sat down next to the Forbes.

"How you feeling, Pastor?" Wayne asked.

"Fine, now."

"Good, this church can't afford to have you lazying around the house." Wayne laughed at his intended joke.

El managed a weak chuckle. He wondered what

would happen if he were disabled. Wayne would probably lead the vote to replace him.

"Bad business." Wayne shook his head.

"Yes, Brother Leroy was a young man," El said.

"No, Pastor, I mean it's bad about Leroy dying, but what he was up to was worse."

El blinked. *What crime was worse than murder?*

Kathy McCarty leaned toward her husband and patted his arm. "Wayne, the pastor doesn't know. How could he?"

"You're right." Wayne squinted slightly as he looked at El. "Well, I've got a friend in the district attorney's office. After they found out about all that money, the Austin police started checking. Leroy was keeping some mighty strange company. I bet one of his so-called buddies bumped him off."

"What kind of strange company?" El suppressed the thought that Jesus could have been accused of keeping strange company.

"Drug dealers." Wayne settled back with the air of a retriever that had just dropped a bird at his master's feet.

El shook his head. "That's bad." Before he could say more Steve leaned over.

"There's Mrs. Boyd and Mrs. Taylor now. I don't know the woman with them."

El stood up. "Must be Mrs. Boyd's mother."

He limped over to them and took Mrs. Boyd's hand. "I'm glad you came tonight." His knee was definitely unhappy.

"I wasn't going to, but Mrs. Taylor said it would be good to get out of the house."

The older woman next to her nodded vigorously. "I agreed."

Mrs. Boyd smiled, then looked at El. "This is my mother, Mrs. West."

"Just call me Barbara, Preacher. Thank y'all for taking care of my little girl."

"We were happy to. Sister Taylor, after you and these folks go through the line come sit with me. I'm over there with Brother Forbes and Brother McCarty."

Mrs. Taylor nodded and ushered her charges through the line. They joined El at the table. He made the necessary introductions, then resumed eating. Kathy McCarty could always be counted on to carry the conversation. He was right.

El finished his dessert and glanced at his watch; six-thirty, time to start the service. He rose.

"I'm sorry ladies, but I've got to start prayer meeting." None of them had finished their meal. "You keep eating. Everyone does."

El tried not to limp as he walked to the lectern set up at one end of the room. From his pocket, he pulled his notes. They included everything from his prayer list to his thoughts on his sermon this coming Sunday.

"Good evening, friends. I'm glad to see you here tonight. I'd like to begin with a prayer. Brother McCarty would you lead us?"

Wayne McCarty nodded happily and stood. He adored public prayer when he did the praying. "Father God . . ."

El heard only his opening. In his mind he went over the evening's lesson. He finished that. His knee ached; he shifted position to ease it. Wayne was still praying. *How does he do that,* El wondered. *He must have been going for five minutes already.* At last came an amen, echoed a little too hardily by the group.

"Thank you, Brother McCarty," El said. "Do we have any prayer concerns to share tonight?"

Several hands went up. El called on them one by one, careful not to skip anyone. He jotted down requests. Mildred Harper's sister was in the hospital for surgery, not specified, which probably meant a hysterectomy. Sister Mildred would never say that in public.

El called on Bo Kavanaugh next. His cousin had been in a car wreck. He'd been hospitalized in San Angelo, but it looked like he was going to be all right.

Finally, El called on Frank Zapalac. Frank sat all alone in the far corner. "My sister's son is going to hell, Pastor. He's been in trouble in school. He really needs to meet the Lord. I'd appreciate prayers for his soul."

El nodded. Frank had told him before about the boy. He suspected it would take more than prayer to set Frank's nephew on the straight and narrow. There were no other hands. Mrs. Boyd had said nothing.

"I want the congregation to remember the Boyds in their loss. The funeral is Friday at ten o'clock at the Oakridge funeral home." El hoped the church turned out for it even if the circumstances were a bit strange.

"Let's pray." El went through the list asking for God's special attention for each. He ended with Leroy. "Amen."

Next, El introduced Mrs. West to the congregation. She smiled, but looked a little uncomfortable. The rest of the prayer meeting passed quickly. Either he explained the lesson well or people weren't very interested because there was little discussion. El let Steve dismiss them with another prayer.

The meeting broke up. El chatted with Bo Kavanaugh about his cousin. His own knee throbbed more every second he stood. El wanted to make an early escape. Bo finally left for choir practice, and El headed for the door.

Wayne McCarty looked like he wanted to speak to El again, but El didn't want to talk to him. He avoided eye contact with Wayne and slipped out the door.

It was still light out. No one else had left yet. Choir practice was one of the major attendance boosters on Wednesday night. Most of those at dinner had choir practice right after prayer meeting, so they stayed, including Wayne. Thank God. "Sorry about that Lord," El added, "but that's how I feel right now."

Something moved over by the arborvitae near the sanctuary. El squinted at the movement. He hoped it wasn't a skunk. No, just an armadillo. It seemed to be digging under the tree. El sighed. He better chase it off before it ruined the trees.

As El limped toward the little armor-plated animal, it continued its grubbing. El grinned. Armadillos couldn't see worth a durn. When he was a kid, he'd sneak up on them and pat them on the back. He hadn't done that in years. He was almost up to the armadillo. El inched forward favoring his knee, then leaned over quickly and patted the creature on the back. It leaped straight in the air and took off. El jumped back, startled despite himself by that defense mechanism, then he laughed.

The armadillo stopped running within a few feet and once more snuffled along, but this time well away from the planted areas. El watched it a moment, then glanced down where it had been digging. There was something shiny there.

El bent over, trying not to flex that bad knee too much. Something glinted in the light from the church. El brushed the dirt away and groped for the object. He picked it up. It was a gun.

El instantly knew which gun, the one that killed Leroy. Why hadn't the sheriff found it? He shrugged, took out a tissue, wrapped the gun in it, and stuck it in his pocket. He'd better call the sheriff. He couldn't go home early after all.

Fifteen minutes later, Deputy Nelson appeared at the church office.

"You found a gun?" Her brown eyes were definitely suspicious.

"Yes," El said and pulled the gun out of his pocket and put it on his desk.

The deputy looked at it, then took a plastic bag out

of her hip pocket. She used her pencil to pick the gun up by the trigger guard and place it in the bag. She closed the bag, then wrote something on the tag attached to it. She left it on the desk in front of her.

"Where?" she asked.

"Under the arborvitae, over by the sanctuary."

"What were you looking for?" There was definitely hostility in the deputy's voice.

El willed himself not to respond to that tone. He described his encounter with the armadillo in detail.

"You ever pet an armadillo, deputy?" El couldn't resist asking.

Deputy Nelson shook her head. "I never had the pleasure. So you chased off the armadillo, then looked at where he'd been digging."

"That's right. I wanted to see if any of the tree roots had been exposed. That's when I saw something shiny."

"So you picked it up."

"Of course."

"Did you ever think that maybe you should call us first?"

"I didn't know what it was until I picked it up."

"Didn't even enter your head, huh?"

"That's right. What are you insinuating?" El didn't understand the deputy's hostility.

"Nothing, Reverend. I suppose you handled it with your bare hands?"

"Of course, I wasn't wearing gloves."

"Were you wearing gloves when you shot him?" Deputy Nelson asked.

El felt like ice water had been poured down his back. The deputy thought he had killed Leroy. He didn't know how to answer.

"Of course not. I mean, I didn't have anything to do with Leroy's death."

"Okay, Reverend, just testing." Deputy Nelson gave a surprisingly disarming grin. "I really don't think you did it, but you've got to admit you shouldn't have picked up the gun. Now, your fingerprints are all over it.''

"I didn't know what it was," El repeated.

"Sure," answered the deputy. "Show me where you found it?" She picked up the bagged gun.

"Okay." El started to rise when a sharp stab of pain in his knee caught him by surprise. He grunted and sat back.

"You okay?" Deputy Nelson asked.

El thought she looked genuinely concerned. "Yeah, my knee just caught me by surprise." He stood up. This time there was no sharp pain, only the familiar ache. "Let's go."

It was dusk outside now. The deputy put the gun in the trunk of her car and took out a large flashlight. Together they walked to where El had found the weapon. Shadows crept out from around the buildings and trees. Even with the lights on around the fellowship hall, the area under the arborvitae was hard to see. Deputy Nelson shone her flashlight on the hole. "There?"

"Yes." El glanced toward fellowship hall. He hoped no one saw them. He watched as the deputy prowled around the trees.

"We'll need to check this in daylight. I'll be right back." She headed back to her car.

Soon she returned with a roll of yellow tape, which she began wrapping around the stand of trees. "Lieutenant Coronado will want to see this in the morning. This should keep the people away."

"But not the armadillos," El couldn't resist saying as the deputy continued her taping. He was glad her back was to him so he couldn't see the deputy's expression.

She finished without comment and returned to her car. She halted by the door. "You'll be here in the morning?"

"Yes."

"Good. Coronado is thorough. He'll want to see you, too. G'night."

El contemplated tomorrow as he watched the patrol car leave. It probably would not be a pleasant day. At least no one inside Fellowship Hall seemed to have noticed the deputy. With luck no one would notice her tape as they left.

"I made a mess of that, didn't I, Lord? I didn't need to antagonize the deputy. She's back to calling me reverend." El limped back to the office and locked it. "Does she really think I did it? Does Coronado? Lord, be with me."

▲7▼

THURSDAY MORNING, EL got to the office before eight o'clock, even Martha was not in yet. When she arrived, her first question was about the yellow tape. He explained briefly, only leaving out the part where the deputy accused him of Leroy's murder. There were probably enough people thinking that anyway. Martha seemed satisfied, and El knew she would happily furnish an explanation to all who inquired.

Coronado arrived at eight-thirty. Martha buzzed El, but the lieutenant didn't wait. He came right into El's office.

El didn't stand. "Good morning," he said. *Two could be impolite. Sorry, Lord.*

"Good morning, Reverend," Coronado replied.

This morning he reminded El of a Mexican bandit in some spaghetti western until El looked into his eyes. Those eyes told El that there was an inner man, one not to underestimate. Suddenly, El remembered that most of those villainous actors in those westerns had been Italian. He suppressed a desire to laugh. He doubted Coronado would see the humor.

"The gun you found killed Leroy Boyd," Coronado said flatly.

El nodded. He had expected that.

"You're not surprised?" Coronado asked.

57

"No, when I saw it was a gun, I figured the murderer must have put it there."

"Good figuring," replied Coronado.

El thought he detected a hint of sarcasm in his voice. Was he still a suspect?

"Tell me about finding the gun, please." Coronado pulled out a small notebook.

"I told the deputy last night."

"I know, but please repeat it for me."

El shrugged. Surely, Coronado had that report. Was he checking to see if El told the same story? El wished he hadn't thought of that. He tried to put that out of his mind as he told Coronado of the incident with the armadillo and the gun. Coronado did not interrupt.

When El finished, Coronado asked, "You have much trouble with armadillos?"

"No, they dig up the lawn once in a while, but that's usually only after we water. Harry, our custodian, tries to water early in the morning." El shrugged. "We have more problems with skunks." He doubted that Coronado cared much about the church's varmint problem.

"I see." Coronado leaned back in his chair. "What did you and Mister Boyd argue about Sunday morning?"

"Argue about?" For a moment, El drew a blank, then he remembered. "Oh, we didn't argue, just had a talk."

"Several people we talked to thought it was an argument."

"Well, Leroy gets, I mean, got pretty emotional about things."

Coronado tilted his head to one side. "What was the talk about?"

"Nothing much," El said.

Coronado's expression hardened.

El went on hurriedly. "We're putting together a new church manual, sort of the governing rules of the church. Our church hasn't revised its manual since it was

formed. With the new families and more members . . .
Well, it was time. One of the changes we were making
had to do with church treasurer. Leroy was our treasurer.'' El looked inquiringly at Coronado. Was this what
he wanted?

"I know. Go on.''

"The new manual would have replaced the treasurer
with a finance committee.''

"Mr. Boyd didn't like that?''

"No, that wasn't it. At least, I don't think so. Leroy
didn't have problems with the committee. He certainly
would have been elected to head it. What he didn't like
was the provision that limited the time of service.'' Of
course, El added to himself, his money-laundering
scheme only worked as long as he was church treasurer.

"Oh.''

"Yes, I, we wanted to get more people involved in
the church. So the manual specified that a member could
only serve on a committee for three years, then they had
to stay off for at least a year. Leroy didn't like that. He'd
been church treasurer for several years and wanted to
continue as treasurer.''

"That's what you argued about?''

"Yes, Leroy blamed me for the changes, said that it
was my fault.'' El stopped.

Coronado said nothing.

"He probably could have gotten the manual changed
if he had really pushed,'' El added. *That would have
been bad. If Leroy had made enough fuss, I might have
been in real trouble with the church. Yet I really had
not thought about it much. Could I have stopped Leroy,
or if push came to shove would I have wanted to? If
being treasurer meant that much to Leroy, then I might
have given in.* El thought again. *Being treasurer had
meant that much to Leroy. Leroy needed to be in charge
to keep using the church to launder all that money.* El sud-

denly felt sick to his stomach. "We agreed to meet Tuesday for lunch to talk some more."

"So the argument was just over church business, not about splitting all that money?"

El started. He hadn't thought that Coronado would think that. "No, I didn't know anything about that money. I told you that already."

"Yes, you did, but you are the only other person authorized to sign checks for the church."

"The pastor was always one of the signers before I came. Someone on staff has to pay the bills, but I never knew about those huge deposits."

"You never called the bank to find out your balance?"

"No. Look, Leroy called me with a running balance every Monday. That was all I needed. Once a month, he forwarded the bank statement to the church."

El thought a moment. "Those statements are on file."

"We checked them yesterday," Coronado answered.

"They are fake, aren't they?" El realized that had to be the answer.

"Yes, it looks like your Mr. Boyd made them out himself. He had a supply of bank forms. We haven't been able to find out where he got them. You have any ideas?"

El shook his head.

"I see." Coronado wrote something in his notebook, then flipped back a couple of pages. "Why would a baptismal robe have pockets?"

El stared at Coronado. That question made no sense. "Baptismal robes don't have pockets."

"One of yours does."

"One of ours?"

"Yes, Deputy Nelson found it the night you were attacked. You gave her the keys to the sanctuary, remember."

"I remember," El said, but actually he did not. He

had found out when he awoke Tuesday that most of Monday night was a blur or simply gone. "But I didn't know we had any robes with pockets. You should check with Steve Forbes or Calvin Roller. Calvin is in charge of the Baptism Committee. Steve works with that committee. Calvin or Steve might know more."

"How do you spell Roller?"

El spelled Calvin's last name for the investigator.

"I'll check with both of them, Pastor. You sure you don't know anything about pockets?"

El shook his head. He had no idea why anyone would need pockets in a baptismal robe. The white cotton garments were simply wraps that a candidate for baptism put on much like a bathrobe. A candidate only wore one for a few minutes. Besides the whole reason for wearing a baptismal robe was because the candidate was going to be dunked. Why put something in a pocket where it would certainly get wet? It made no sense.

"Well, thanks." Coronado stood up.

El rose this time.

"I may need to ask you some more questions. You'll be around?"

"Yes, of course."

"Good."

El watched Coronado leave. Did the man believe El killed Leroy? *I hope not, Lord.*

At ten-fifteen, Martha came to his door. "Mr. Nabors rescheduled for today at ten-thirty. Remember?"

El did not, but he smiled and nodded at Martha. He spent the next few minutes clearing his desk.

Jack Nabors showed up precisely at ten-thirty. El only knew him slightly. He and his wife were regulars on Sunday morning but rarely came any other time. Jack was just under six feet, gray-headed, and putting on a little weight. Nadine was tall for a woman, trim and dark-haired. She looked younger than Jack. They made a nice couple. El frowned. He hadn't seen Nadine last Sunday, just Jack. *What was wrong?* Martha showed Jack in, and shut the door behind him.

El stood and shook his hand. "Good to see you, Jack. Sorry you couldn't make it Monday, but it was just as well."

"So it seems," Jack said and eased himself into the chair next to El's desk.

El came around his desk and sat in the other chair. "What can I do for you?" El had no idea why Jack Nabors wanted to see him. He had not told Martha anything when he called last week except that it was personal.

"Nadine told me to come talk to you." Jack looked at his feet.

El waited.

After a full minute of silence, Jack said, "She's going to leave me." He did not raise his head.

Jack had a bald patch, El noticed as he stared at his bowed head. "Why?"

Jack shook his head. "It's no big deal. I've been having a little fling, but I still love her."

"A little fling?"

Jack looked up and grinned. "Yep, with that Mary Lynn that sings in the choir."

"You're having an affair with Mary Lynn Reeves?"

"It's not an affair. We just like each other, like doing things together. My wife just doesn't understand."

"Have you been intimate?" Jack's confession had not surprised El much, but Mary Lynn's involvement had.

"Of course."

El closed his eyes for a moment, then looked straight in Jack's eyes and said, "You're a married man, that's adultery. A sin."

"Now, Preacher, you know men have our needs. I don't think you need to label it like that."

"What about your wife? Has she denied your needs?"

El wryly noted that he and Jack both used a euphemism.

"Well, no, she's still willing, but it's not the same as with Mary Lynn." There was that grin again.

"Jack," El said, "I can't condone this. You took vows when you married. You're a good Christian. You've got to drop Mary Lynn. Stick to your wife."

"I knew you'd say that. You've never been married. You don't understand. Do you even know..." Jack rose abruptly. His chair scraped the floor and made an abrasive chirping sound. "I'm sorry, Pastor. This isn't going to work."

Before El could say more, Jack turned and strode to the door. He opened it and left without a backward glance.

El didn't go after him. He'd have to try to talk with Mrs. Nabors and perhaps Mary Lynn. How would he approach Mary Lynn Reeves? He didn't want to drive her away from the church. For that matter, he didn't want to drive Jack Nabors away. As long as someone came to church, El figured he had a chance to reach that person.

"Dear Lord, this is one for you. Help me to guide this man back to his wife. Amen."

El looked at his watch. He could leave a little early, grab some lunch, then make the nursing-home visit he had missed Monday. *Yes, that's what I'll do.*

A little after one, he reached the nursing home in South Austin where Mary Ann Black, a longtime church member, now lived. At the entrance to the nursing home, El paused. This place with its unkempt occupants and smell of urine always depressed him. Besides, Sister Mary Ann was always critical. Critical of him, the church, the world around her. El squared his shoulders. Better get it over with.

The interior of the building was just as before, brown and gray carpet, gray, vinyl-coated walls. El wrinkled his nose as he walked down the hall. One elderly woman with a walker inched her way down the corridor. El smiled at her, but she only stared vacantly ahead. He reached Sister Mary Ann's room and knocked at her door.

"Come in," she said in a voice that belied her ninety-eight years.

El went in. "Good afternoon, Sister Mary Ann. How are you?"

Sister Mary Ann sat in her bed wearing an old cotton duster faded almost to white. "Oh, Pastor, not so good. This place doesn't have decent food. You know, I got false teeth, and they don't work so good. So what do these fools do? Give me tough meat."

"I'm sorry to hear that." El had learned over the course of many visits not to take her complaints too seriously.

She peered at him as if he were a prize steer. "You're too thin." She reached out and squeezed his upper arm. "You got to eat more. What you need to do is get married. A wife would fatten you up."

"Now, Sister Mary Ann, you know I don't even have a girlfriend."

"Umm. Well, you should get one."

"You're probably right."

"I've been listening to your sermons," she said.

"Good, I'm glad you do." The church taped all the services, then provided copies to shut-ins. He sometimes suspected that Sister Mary Ann was the only one who listened to them. He knew she did because she usually disagreed with him.

"You're way too namby-pamby. You have to make people fear the devil. They've got to know that if they don't accept Christ and obey him, then they're condemned to hellfire."

"Sister Mary Ann, I try to make people want to follow Christ, not scare them into it."

"That's silly," she said. "Get them anyway you can.

In my day, people knew what happened to sinners. You should preach that.''

El nodded. He knew about Sister Mary Ann's beliefs. When she was a young woman, she'd had her own sister kicked out of the small, rural church southeast of Austin where they both belonged. Her sister's crime: She had danced with her own husband one Saturday at a picnic. Well, standards had been different seventy years ago.

He spent a few minutes more with her as she went through her list of complaints against her family. Finally, El said a brief prayer and left.

Next, he went to see Mildred Harper's sister. She was doing fine recovering from a hysterectomy just as El had guessed. Margaret was very different from Mildred. El actually enjoyed his visit.

El got back to church just before three-thirty. He had just settled behind his desk when the phone rang.

Martha said, ''There's a caller on the line that won't give his name.''

''That's okay,'' El said. He was used to people not wanting the church staff to know they needed to talk to the pastor. Maybe it was Jack Nabors.

''Hello, this is Eldon Littlejohn. Can I help you?''

''You sure can, Pastor.'' The voice on the other end of the line sounded muffled, disguised.

''How?'' A shiver of excitement ran down El's spine.

''We need the stuff you made for Leroy.''

El nodded to himself. That voice had made him think that this call had something to do with the killing. ''What stuff?''

''Don't jerk us around, Pastor. You know, the stuff you've been cooking up for Leroy. He told us you were his supplier.''

''Then he lied,'' El answered.

''Maybe, maybe. We'll be in touch.'' The man hung up.

El put the receiver down slowly. Stuff, it didn't take

much imagination to realize that was some sort of drug. Leroy told them he was the supplier. *Why?*

He realized what he must do. He found the card Coronado had given him this morning and dialed the number. Coronado himself answered.

Quickly, El recounted his conversation. When he finished, there was only silence at the other end of the line.

"What do you think?" El asked, exasperated after the silence continued.

"Why did they call you, Reverend?"

"I told you I don't know. Just that Leroy must have told them I was his supplier."

"Were you?"

"No." El felt the flush of anger. He took a deep breath. He suspected that Coronado was trying to get him angry, to say something intemperate. He was close to succeeding.

"All right, Reverend. Thanks for calling. We'll be in touch."

After he hung up, El thought about Coronado's reaction. He had not seemed very surprised. *What was going on?* El shook his head. He better not think about that now. Tomorrow was Leroy's funeral, and El had to deliver the message. He went back to work, but his mind kept straying. Finally, at a quarter to five, he gave up. He'd finish at home.

He turned on the radio as he drove home. The news came on. El didn't pay much attention until he heard the announcer say that Marcus Matthew Depew had made a speech denouncing the current invasion of violence into every institution, even the church. El turned up the volume as the senator began to speak.

"Evil has invaded all areas of our society. Even now violence has found its way into our most sacred institution, the church. Just this week, violence led to the death of a respected member of a Baptist church here in Austin. This is a result of the permissiveness of this world. I don't know, but I suspect that if you check on what was preached in that church you will find that it was not the Bible, but instead the ways of the world disguised as truth. There is only one . . .''

El switched off the radio. He wanted to throw up. Depew was talking about his church. How dare he say that El had not been preaching the Bible. El stopped the car in his driveway. He leaned his head on the steering wheel. Depew's words materialized his worst fear, that somehow his ministry had failed, that he was responsible for what had happened.

El straightened up. This did no good. He got out and headed for the steps. He really didn't preach the Bible, at least not as that lawmaker meant. Because . . . Because El did not believe in it as that man did. No, El believed that it was the record of God's work in this world, but it was a record made by fallible men. He never preached that, but that view colored his sermons. It had gotten him in trouble more than once at his previous churches. It might get him in trouble at Hill Country, too, because most members of his congregation believed as that senator, that the Bible was the infallible Word of God, which to them meant it contained absolutely no error.

Maybe he should have joined another denomination where he would be on the conservative side instead of the liberal one, but he had been raised a Baptist. His parents were lifelong members of the largest Southern Baptist church in Austin. When God's call came, he had assumed that it was to be a Southern Baptist minister. He trudged up the steps favoring his knee. At least it seemed to be getting better.

Once inside, El flopped down on his sofa. He was back where he always seemed to wind up, wondering if he had made the correct decision when he entered the ministry.

''Dear Lord, I'm sorry to bother you again with the

same old problem, but I have such doubts. I don't believe as many of my congregation do. Why couldn't you make it clear what to believe? Why make it so hard? Oh, Lord, give me strength. Amen.''

▲8▼

EL WOKE EARLY. This morning he had to do Leroy's funeral. He fixed an instant breakfast and gulped it down while he listened to the morning news. There was nothing new and no mention of Leroy's murder. Back in his bedroom, he dressed slowly, going over the message he had composed last night. A message for the living, not the dead. As usual, he found himself praying as he finished. "Oh, Lord, I'm afraid. Afraid I won't reach those that need to hear and afraid I'll offend those who don't need the message. Amen."

El headed out the door, but he stopped at the head of the porch steps. He leaned against the railing. "Lord, I'm afraid for myself, too. I don't want to be arrested for something I didn't do. Be with me."

El got to the funeral home shortly before nine. As always he noted the unidentifiable smell that seemed to permeate every funeral home. Formaldehyde and death.

The director greeted him warmly. "Pastor Littlejohn, you're looking well. Would you like to see the body?"

El wanted to say no, instead he nodded.

The director ushered him to the front of the chapel. The casket stood to the right of center. El noticed the abundance of flowers. Bouquets hung from the wall and large, free-standing wreaths and sprays were arrayed at either end of the casket. Red roses draped the casket itself. *Were any of those arrangements from Leroy's confederates in crime?* El put that thought out of his mind as he looked at Leroy.

Leroy lay on a bed of pearl gray satin, dressed in a dark gray suit. El stared at the body. Leroy looked more striking today than he ever had alive. The undertaker had done a good job. Leroy's expression was pleasant, almost serene.

El closed his eyes. "We all sin and fall short," he whispered. He only hoped that Leroy had truly known Jesus.

El turned back to the funeral director who stood at a discreet distance. "Thanks," El said.

Together they walked to the far left to the waiting room behind the chapel. No one was there yet. They stood in the doorway, so they could see the entrance to the chapel. The director briefly laid out the schedule and arrangements at the cemetery. El listened absently. When the director finished, he excused himself. El remained where he was.

At nine, El noticed the first attendees arrive. He moved into the waiting room as the funeral director greeted these first arrivals. El pulled his notes from his pocket and went over them again. Usually he did not prepare as much for a funeral, but somehow this one seemed to need it. He finished going over the notes, then glanced at his wristwatch, nine-fifteen.

The door at the rear of the waiting room opened, and Melanie Boyd, the children, and Mrs. Wood entered accompanied by a funeral-home employee. El went to Melanie Boyd. She looked very pale. *Was it just the effect of the black dress she wore?*

"Sister Melanie, how are you doing?"

Melanie Boyd smiled slightly, but her eyes didn't. "I'm fine, Brother El. As soon as this is over, the kids and I are going home with mother."

"To Dallas?"

Melanie Boyd nodded. "Yes, I want to get the children away from here. I'll be back next week by myself."

El nodded in return. "It's probably best, but we'll miss you at church."

"You might, Pastor, but I don't think many others will."

Was there a hint of bitterness in her tone? "Sister Melanie . . ." El was about to tell her that wasn't true when he thought better of it. *Had anything specific been said or done,* he wondered. He must find a way to know for sure.

Organ music swelled through the chapel. El patted Melanie's hand, took Mrs. Wood's and squeezed, then walked into the chapel, past the coffin, and sat down in one of the two chairs against the wall a few feet behind the podium. Behind him the organ music grew louder. The organ, its player, and any singers were hidden from view by a section of wall.

The music continued as people continued to enter. El was surprised how many. At least half were from church. El wondered if they were truly sympathetic or just curious. "Sorry, Lord. Sometimes I'm too cynical," he said under his breath.

Lieutenant Coronado, dressed in a dark blue suit, entered the chapel. El was not surprised. Another taller, younger man appeared to be with him. They took a seat discreetly in the rear.

El surveyed the audience. There were a number of men in business suits who El had never before seen. *Business associates of Leroy's?* El wondered. *Which business?*

The organ grew louder. Steve Forbes began to sing the first hymn. El always found this disembodied singing strange. Why conceal the source of the music? Steve finished. El stood up; now it was his turn.

"Let us pray. Lord, we are here today to say goodbye to Brother Leroy. You know our hearts are sad that he died so young. Be with us in our grief and give comfort to us and especially Leroy's family. Amen.''

El surveyed the crowd before he continued. Not many tears.

"Leroy Woodrow Boyd was born February 19, 1942. He died July 31, 1988. He is survived by his wife, Melanie Ann Boyd, and his two children, Heather Meredith Boyd and Jason Joseph Boyd. He will be interred at the Oakridge Cemetery."

Finished with the ritual recital, El sat down. Once again, Steve's voice seemed to float in as he sang another solemn hymn. The music had an effect. Several in the crowd began to wipe their eyes. El understood. Some hymns evoked memories of the past, of loss, of other funerals. Steve finished.

El stood and returned to the podium. "I've known Leroy ever since I came to Hill Country. He was a God-fearing man." El heard his audience shift in their seats. *They don't believe that. Well, I do. Just because a man did evil didn't mean he didn't fear God.* El continued, telling personal experiences he had had with Leroy.

Finally, he came to the point he knew everyone had been waiting for. "Brother Leroy sinned. We know that. In man's eyes, he sinned pretty badly, but it is not for man to judge. God will judge. All we need to remember is that Jesus died for us that our sins might be forgiven. I think that even includes the sins of Brother Leroy. So I say to you who knew the same Brother Leroy I did, to remember that Leroy."

El ended with another prayer and then sat down. There were very few tissues in evidence. El's sermon had not moved them as the music had.

The funeral director came down front. "Any of you who wish to may view the body."

Soon a slow line was moving past the coffin. A few people left the line to say a word to Melanie Boyd. El saw Alice Taylor do that. *Bless her,* he thought. As she

passed him, he noticed how red-rimmed her eyes were.
This had certainly upset her.

A couple of men walked by. They hardly glanced at
the coffin, but they stared at El. El suddenly wondered
if one of these had been his caller.

Most of the rest that passed El knew from church.
Some nodded to him as they walked by. Wayne Mc-
Carty shook his head as he passed. El hoped that Sister
Melanie hadn't seen him. The last mourner was a
stranger to El. When he left the chapel, the director es-
corted Melanie Boyd to the casket. El was glad to see
she had sense enough to leave the children with her
mother.

He stepped to her side as she turned away from the
coffin. "I really do believe that he was saved, Sister
Melanie."

"Thank you," she whispered.

El headed for his car. He would drive himself to the
cemetery. After speaking to the director, he left ahead
of the procession.

The director had given him directions to the grave site
at the cemetery. El found it without difficulty. He stood
under the green tent erected by the funeral home as he
waited the arrival of the funeral procession. The shade
was welcome in the August heat. Already his shirt stuck
to his back, wet with sweat. El stared at the empty grave.
Artificial grass had been spread around it hiding the raw
edges. The machinery for lowering the casket was in
place above the empty hole. El looked away, that hole
bothered him.

Something moved over by a clump of cedar. El peered
at the trees. He caught a glimpse of an arm. Probably
just a caretaker. He couldn't see anyone now.

The crunch of tires on gravel announced the arrival
of the hearse with its procession from the funeral home.
El watched as the casket was unloaded and brought over
to the grave. While the men set it in place, El glanced

at the cedars again. He could barely make out the shape
of a man behind them. El resisted the urge to walk over
to the trees and see who was so shy. People filed in
slowly. Melanie Boyd and her mother arrived. Leroy had
no other living relatives. His parents had been killed in
a car wreck along with a brother when Leroy was in
college. El went to speak to Melanie and Mrs. West
again, but he couldn't resist a quick peek at the cedars.
The skulker was gone. El studied the crowd. *Had he
joined it?*

After speaking to Melanie and her mother, El returned
to the grave side. He gave a brief prayer, and said a few
words about eternal life. All the while he studied the
crowd. There were some of the same strangers from the
funeral chapel. *Was there someone new in the rear?* El
could not be sure.

As the people walked by Melanie and her family, El
tried to get a better look. Yes, there was someone new,
a tall, thin man dressed in a cream-colored jacket and
pants. Of course, the man could have been at the funeral
home, and El had just not seen him. The man walked
nearer. He nodded to El as he passed. The stranger spoke
to Melanie Boyd then left.

El had no more time to think about mysteries. He had
to be back at the office. Quickly, he said his good-byes
and left.

El's morning appointment had canceled, he found out
when he reached the office. He had no others. El fumed.
He could have stayed at the cemetery and found out who
the strangers were, especially the tall man. "Sorry, Lord.
I know that it's none of my business." El set to work
on his sermon for Sunday. He had to get his mind off
the cemetery.

He succeeded. Soon he was totally absorbed. Some-
time later, he heard someone clear his throat. El had not
heard his door open, but Steve Forbes stood in the door-

way. There was a funny expression on his face.

"Come in, Steve," El said.

"I'm not disturbing you?" Steve asked.

El shook his head. It was true. He had just finished the last sentence of Sunday's sermon. It would be better if he waited a while before revising.

"I talked with a few of our members after the service."

"Oh." El felt the hair on the back of his neck prickle. *Something was up for sure.*

Steve looked at the desktop.

Bad sign, El thought.

"Yes," Steve said. "A couple of deacons and some other church members."

"Well," El prompted. He wished Steve would get to the point. His stomach was already getting queasy.

"They didn't like your message at the funeral. They thought that you should have condemned Brother Leroy's actions more."

"In front of the man's wife and kids?" El didn't understand his fellow Christians sometimes.

Steve looked at him. "I understand. I'm just telling you what was said."

"You going to tell me who said it?"

Steve shook his head. "I promised not to."

"I see." El wondered what Steve had thought of the sermon. "What else did they have to say."

"A couple of them felt you should have said something about backsliding Christians. But most questioned whether Brother Leroy was saved. They all thought you should have said that he wasn't."

El was not surprised. Most churchgoers believed the Baptist doctrine of once saved, always saved. To them, Leroy's actions were evidence that he had never been saved. El sighed. He believed a man could lose his salvation only if he turned his back on God deliberately. If any of those good Baptists found out he did not believe in once saved, always saved, he'd be out the door in a moment. *Had Leroy rejected God?* El thought not.

"That's really not for us to say," El said.

"I don't know," Steve answered.

El raised an inquiring eyebrow. He had not expected that from Steve.

"I mean," Steve said, "Not that we can know, but some behavior is so bad it makes you wonder. If we don't condemn it, won't that hurt others worse?"

El leaned back. "You know the answer, Steve. Condemn the sin, not the sinner. Sometimes though it's hard to distinguish, I know. But I really think one of our jobs is to assure the living that they can't do anything so bad that God won't forgive them."

Steve nodded slowly. "You're right, Pastor. Just forget what I said."

El smiled and nodded, too, but he noticed that Steve's expression was not one of agreement, and Steve had called him pastor. He rarely did that. It seemed to put a barrier between them. Steve was more conservative than he, but it hadn't mattered before. Did it now?

Steve left. El had trouble getting back to work. Had he said the right thing? Usually, he didn't worry about what he said in front of a coworker, but . . . El closed his eyes. *Get back to work now,* he told himself. The sermon lay in front of him. He would polish it.

At three-thirty, Martha rang. Deputy Nelson was here to see him. El was struck by the coincidence. His mysterious call yesterday had been at this time.

Deputy Nelson looked more formidable than before, El thought, as she entered. Her expression was set and her eyes hostile.

"Lieutenant Coronado asked me to drop by. There's some questions we need answered."

"Sure," El said although he could not think of anything Coronado had failed to ask.

"The lab report came in on that baptismal robe with pockets I found. There was a white powder in one of the pockets."

El's heartbeat quickened. Had Leroy used the robe for an illicit purpose? If so, maybe Steve Forbes had been right. To use God's house . . . "A white powder?"

Deputy Nelson nodded and pulled out her notebook. "3-methylfentanyl."

"Synthetic heroin, China White," El said as his stomach turned queasy. Drugs in the Lord's House.

"How did you know that?" Nelson asked.

El shrugged. "My undergraduate degree was in chemistry. I've kept up a little. Somewhere I read about the synthetic heroins, that 3-methylfentanyl had been passed off as a very pure Southeast Asian heroin, called China White."

Deputy Nelson was writing in her notebook. "Could you make it?"

El shook his head. "No, not unless I had the synthesis. I don't have any idea of where to start."

"But if you had the way to make it, say written down for you, you could?"

"Of course, I told you I have a chemistry degree, but that doesn't mean I would." El wondered if he looked as green as he felt. He wanted to throw up. "Was Leroy making that stuff?"

The deputy looked at El for what seemed a long time to him before she answered. "Probably not. Everything we know suggests that Leroy was the middleman. Someone else was making the drug, and Leroy was delivering it to whoever distributed it. The DPS chemist told me that stuff was real pure. He said it would take someone with more than average skill to make it that pure. A chemist, probably."

El suddenly felt cold. Had the deputy known his background before she came? Had this been a trick to see if he would lie? He no longer felt sick, just afraid.

"Well, I haven't been in a lab in ten years. I certainly didn't make it."

"I didn't say you did, Reverend. Is there anyone in your congregation with those kind of skills?"

"In my congregation?" El's queasiness returned. If the deputy was right, someone in his congregation made the drug for Leroy. In his church. *Dear Lord, evil so close.*

The deputy nodded encouragingly.

"I can't think of anyone. As far as I know I'm the only one with a chemistry background."

The deputy stood up. The corners of her mouth quivered upward. "As far as we know, too. Thank you, Reverend."

El did not even rise as she left. He was too stunned. The deputy had known; she'd been testing him. El shut his eyes. That must mean he was a suspect. He could see the headlines now: BAPTIST MINISTER ARRESTED FOR MURDER!

Stay calm, he told himself. You're innocent. He remembered all the recent stories about innocent men sent to Texas prisons. He did not want to be one of those. If the sheriff decided he needed an arrest . . . El opened his eyes. This was wrong. He was a minister; he should have more faith.

"Dear Lord, I'm scared. Give me strength, please. Help me, Lord."

El knew what he needed to do, but he didn't want to do it. The deacons and trustees had to be told. First, though, he had better tell Steve. El got up. Steve's office was adjacent to his, his door was to the side of Martha's desk instead of behind it as was El's. Steve's door was closed. El knocked.

"Come in," Steve said.

El's expression must have alerted Steve.

"What's wrong?" he asked.

El dropped into the chair in front of Steve's desk. He took a deep breath, then told Steve about Coronado's visit yesterday, the baptismal robes, Deputy Nelson's visit today, and the drugs.

"Drugs in a baptismal robe," Steve whispered.

"I know, it's bad. We better call the deacons and trustees. They need to know what the sheriff has found so far."

Steve nodded. "Listen, why don't you let me do that. You've got enough going on."

El thought for a moment. "Okay, except for Brother Wayne, I'll call him. If anyone wants to talk to me, put them through."

Steve nodded.

El returned to his office and called Wayne McCarty. To his surprise, he got him. Briefly, he explained it all to Wayne.

"Damnation, Pastor. Things only get worse. First Brother Leroy, now there must be somebody else. This sure isn't going to help our church."

"I know, Brother Wayne, I know."

"Well, thanks for telling me. I'm going to check with my friend in the DA's office, see if he has any info. I'll get back to you if he does."

"Thanks, Brother Wayne."

"Good-bye."

▲9▼

SUNDAY DAWNED WARM and bright without a cloud in the sky. El watched the sun rise as he sipped his morning coffee. He had slept fitfully and now was up earlier than usual, even for a Sunday. Yesterday, he had polished his sermon, then worked on the Sunday School lesson for the men's class he taught between services. No one had interrupted his day. Alone with his thoughts, he often found himself going over and over the events of the past week. Now, he realized he was doing that again.

Could he have prevented Leroy's death? El walked out onto the deck. He had to believe there was nothing he could have done. Then came the other question. Should he have known about the money laundering? The drugs. Probably not. Leroy's handling of church finances had started long before El came to Hill Country, and no one would have suspected that drugs were being exchanged inside a church. Still . . .

El sighed and looked toward the east. His cabin might be small, but you couldn't beat the view out over the hills. A haze blurred the edges of the farthest hills. The nearest ones were robed in dark green unbroken even by a deer trail, while the ones beyond faded into washed-denim blue. Something moved nearby. He heard the rustle of dry grass. There, at the edge of his yard, a portly

skunk sauntered toward the brush. Its black and white
tail flared horizontally behind the sleek body. El smiled,
that skunk was going home to its den for the day, satisfied after a night of foraging. Perhaps the world was
not so bad after all.

An hour and a half later, shortly before eight, El
pulled into the church parking lot. Only a few cars were
there at this hour. The day was already warming up. The
morning breeze had an undercurrent of heat. El headed
for his office. He always spent a few minutes there before the early worship service.

Another vehicle pulled into the parking lot. El
stopped. He recognized Bill Gunter's car. El tried to ignore the feeling of unease that car created. He hadn't
talked to Gunter since Monday; he didn't want to now,
but there was no way to avoid the man. El watched
Gunter get out and walk toward him. This morning he
looked more like a department store mannequin than
ever.

''Brother Littlejohn, I'm glad to see you're getting
around okay.'' Bill Gunter said as he came up beside
El.

Not pastor, El noted, but brother. *What was the matter
now?*

''I'm doing fine. My knee is just about well.''

''Glad to hear that.'' Gunter put his arm around El's
shoulders as they walked toward the church office. That
gesture was meant to reassure El, instead it made him
more wary. He fought the desire to pull away.

''You know this is really bad business, this money
laundering and drugs,'' Gunter said.

El nodded.

''We need to keep the church out of it as much as
possible,'' Gunter patted El's shoulder as he spoke.
''Whoever else is involved, I hope he has the decency
not to drag the church down. If it were me, I'd just take

my letter now, before I was arrested, so I wouldn't even be a member.''

"Let's pray that no one else in our church is involved," El said. But Bill Gunter was correct. There had to be someone else from the church in on the drug deal. Why else use the baptismal robes?

Bill patted El on the back again. "I sure will, but it sure looks like Leroy wasn't in the drug deal alone. He might have been doing the money by himself, but not dope. But maybe you're right. Maybe someone from outside the church snuck in during the week, and Leroy just picked the dope up on Sunday. I'm probably worrying about nothing. It's not likely anyone in this church knows enough to make dope. Huh?''

El wondered if Bill were testing him. *Did Bill know that I was a chemist?*

"No, it's not likely," El answered.

"Well, I'll see you later, Brother Littlejohn." Bill gave him a pat on the back and turned toward the education building.

El walked toward the office, his early-morning serenity destroyed. A sour taste filled his mouth, and his stomach burned. He was sure that Bill Gunter meant him when he spoke of that member not bringing the church down. Resign, that was what Bill really meant. Resign, before you are arrested.

The air conditioning was off when El entered the church office, and it was stifling. El switched on the unit, then headed for his own office. He locked the door behind him and dropped into a chair.

"Oh, Lord, my own people think I'm guilty. What am I going to do?"

El slumped forward in the chair and put his head in his hands. He couldn't even pray anymore. God didn't seem to be listening.

Time passed. El's thoughts scurried through his mind like fire ants in search of food.

At last El straightened. "Dear Lord, I call myself a minister, but I don't even have enough faith to talk to you." El took a deep breath. "Lord, you know how it is with me. Maybe I don't have the proper reverence. I don't get down on my knees to you. But Lord, I do honor you. Please give me strength. Amen."

The prayer did bring a measure of relief. El glanced at his watch. It was almost time for the first service. He needed to think of the congregation, not himself, now. He stood, straightened his tie, opened the door, and headed toward the sanctuary.

The organ music had started when he entered the sanctuary. There was no choir at this service. Attendance at the eight-thirty service was always sparse, but a faithful few came every Sunday, and since it was summer, some came who wanted to get out of church early. El counted. Thirty-two. Better than usual, but no new faces.

The service went without a hitch. El always thought of this service as a chance to practice his sermon for the real service at eleven. He knew that meant he made this service more casual, but the attendees seemed to like it, El had received no complaints. No one came forward at the invitation, the norm for the early service. Most people who wanted to join the church did so at eleven o'clock.

After the early service, El grabbed a cup of coffee from the pot in the foyer, said hello to a few church members, then went to his Sunday School class. Sometimes, El envied ministers of larger churches who only preached on Sundays. Today's lesson was from Ezra on trusting God. How appropriate.

The class was full, but no visitors. There were ten men: Bill Gunter, Otis Wheeler, Wayne McCarty, Frank Zapalac, Henry Wieland, Ralph Leonard, Jim Creamer, Chuck Downing, Russell Booker, and Homer Adams. Leroy Boyd had been a members of this class. Good men for the most part, even Bill Gunter for all El's problems with him, although Ralph had played around in his younger days, and Henry had gotten in some scrapes with the law. Now, they were all pillars of the church. Sort of. El suspected that Ralph still fancied himself a ladies' man and Jim, a loan officer, had little compassion for others. But in Sunday School, they were just a bunch of old friends getting a chance to visit and study the Bible together.

El struggled through the lesson. At least Bill Gunter made no reference to their earlier conversation. El was not much of an Old Testament scholar, and the teacher's manual had not been enlightening, but the class members helped out. The men supplied their own thoughts on Ezra, and El didn't have to talk the whole time.

Just before class ended, El asked Otis Wheeler to teach next week. El had one of the members of the class teach as often as he dared. Right now, he needed a breather from teaching, especially Old Testament. Besides, he couldn't help but think that he might be under arrest by next week. Otis agreed reluctantly. Otis was actually a gifted teacher; he just didn't see himself as one. Otis would do a good job on Ezra.

The eleven o'clock service had started when El took his place. The choir and congregation were singing the first hymn. The choir's formal maroon and white robes always reminded El of bigger churches, but both the choir members and the congregation liked them. El looked out over the congregation searching for new faces, checking to see that familiar ones weren't missing.

El's heartbeat quickened. There was Lieutenant Coronado near the back of the sanctuary. On the left side, El saw some new faces, two men. He kept his gaze moving, but he came back to them. Yes, they had been at the funeral service yesterday. The hymn finished, and Steve Forbes came to the pulpit to give a prayer and welcome visitors.

El bent his head as Steve prayed, but he didn't pay

attention to his words. All he could think of was those strangers and Coronado. *Maybe, they were together. Not from the sheriff's department, but from the city. Or the feds?* El swallowed hard. He wondered just how big an operation Leroy had been involved in. Of course, those two might be what he first suspected, members of Leroy's drug ring.

Luckily, El heard Steve's "amen" and raised his head on cue. Steve was now welcoming visitors. The ushers were standing at the front ready to go down each aisle and hand out visitor packets. Steve asked the visitors to please raise their hands so the ushers could find them. There were more hands up than usual. El was sure some were people who had been at the funeral.

El watched Otis Wheeler passing out the packets. When Otis reached the left rear he sort of jumped. El tried to see who was there. The person was hidden by Mrs. Pierson's hat. Mrs. Pierson always wore a big hat. "To protect my complexion, Pastor."

The person leaned toward Otis to get his packet. A man. El blinked. He recognized the man, just as Otis had. Marcus Matthew Depew. *Good Lord! What was he doing here?*

Steve had finished. "All rise for hymn number one hundred and seven, 'There Is a Fountain.'"

El stood. As he sang, he tried to get a glimpse of Depew again, but Mrs. Pierson's hat was an effective screen.

Steve kept the congregation on its feet for the doxology, then the ushers began to collect the morning offering. El turned his mind to his sermon. After the offering, the choir would sing, then it would be his turn. El enjoyed the choir. He missed it during early service.

"Dear Lord, I need your strength this morning. Let me bring a message these people will hear. Lord, let me forget myself and my fears. Amen." El thought of something else. "Sorry, Lord, but why is that man here today?'' *Probably to check my theology,* El added to himself. ''Lord, I just don't understand how he can be your servant when he trashes so many people's lives. Sorry. I know, it's not for me to judge.''

The choir began to sing. El noticed that Coronado was surveying the crowd much as El had done. Coronado looked straight at El and smiled. El felt like a field mouse mesmerized by a rattler. He tried to follow the words of the song the choir was singing. He could not; he kept returning to look at Coronado who now had his head down. *Reading something? Writing something?*

The choir finished. Now, it was El's turn to speak. He willed himself to walk slowly to the pulpit. He spread out his notes, then asked the congregation to pray with him. That finished, he began his sermon. To his relief, it went smoothly.

El finished by inviting people to come forward to join the church. He nodded to Steve who started the hymn of invitation. El went down the steps to stand in front of the pulpit to greet anyone who came forward. For him, this was the most awkward part of the service. In a church the size of Hill Country, someone came forward about one Sunday in five, so most of the time he had nothing to do but to stand and look solemn.

This Sunday appeared to be another lonesome one. He was about to signal Steve to stop after the next verse when movement caught his eye. It was not someone coming forward. Senator Depew was leaving early.

El turned to Steve and nodded. Steve nodded in return with a slight frown. Steve figured that one of their problems was that El kept the invitation too short. El suspected that Steve would have them sing all the verses of that hymn at least three times if El allowed it. The hymn ended.

Steve moved to the pulpit to give the closing prayer. As he began to pray, El walked to the rear of the church.

He stationed himself just outside the vestibule door. Steve was still praying. El glanced around the parking lot. Depew was just pulling out. The man had a driver, he sat in the back seat of a Lincoln Town Car. As the car turned Depew looked directly at El. El had never seen such an expression of malice. Then the car accelerated and was gone. El swallowed. Why did that man care about him? El shook his head. Maybe he'd been wrong about that look. *Maybe.*

El had no more time to think about it, the church was emptying. El spent the next few minutes shaking hands and saying meaningless pleasantries. Jack Nabors came out without his wife or Mary Lynn. He shook El's hand.

"Good sermon," Jack said.

"Thanks," El answered. "Jack, we need to talk some more. Call. Will you?"

"Maybe, Pastor, maybe," Jack said, then walked off.

El tried to think of a way to reach the man. He'd have to call Jack if Jack didn't call him by Wednesday.

Alice Taylor's gentle touch on his arm brought him back to his duties.

"Sister Alice, good to see you."

"You, too, Pastor. I've been praying for you."

"Thank you," El said. He was sure there were tears in her eyes. El didn't have time to say anything else as more people filed by.

The strangers from the local funeral left without shaking hands. Most people were gone when Coronado came out. He reached out and shook El's hand.

"Good sermon, Pastor. Maybe I'll come again."

"You do that." El suspected his smile looked strained. He resisted the temptation to ask Coronado why he had come today. The officer nodded and walked away.

In minutes, the parking lot was almost deserted. A few people had stopped to chat, but most left immediately either to get home or more likely to beat the Presbyterians to the cafeteria. El was about to leave, too, when Steve appeared.

"Did you see who was in the congregation?" he said excitedly.

El shook his head. Who did Steve mean?

"Marcus Depew. He left early, but he was here. Wouldn't it be great if he joined?"

El nodded. "Sure, but a state senator like him is not likely to join a church out here." Besides, El mused, after the look I got, I don't think the man planned on joining Hill Country.

Steve frowned at El. "He lives out this way. He might make this his church home while he is in Austin."

"I don't think so. He's more likely to join either First or Hyde Park."

"Well, you never know. He might want to be in a smaller church."

Suddenly, El didn't want to talk about Depew anymore, and it bothered him that Steve thought the man would be an asset to their church.

"Maybe. I'll see you later," El answered. He hurried down the steps and went straight to his Mustang.

As he pulled out of the parking lot he remembered Depew's expression. El shook his head.

"Lord, what did I do? Does he know I'm a liberal?" Right now being labeled a liberal among Southern Baptists might torpedo any future job opportunities. "You know I might be a liberal as far as Baptists are concerned, God, but that's not very liberal in the real world. I just don't think you bothered to dictate scripture. I think you give us more credit than that. But even if I'm wrong, Lord, I hope you won't be mad." *That's it,* he thought, *cover all your bases, even with God.* "Sorry, Lord, I'll try to do better."

"Doubt if I will," El added a moment later.

▲10▼

ALOUD BANGING awakened El. He grabbed his clock and blinked at it. Seven-thirty. He realized someone was pounding on his front door. Who would be here this early? A church emergency could be phoned. He grabbed his robe from the foot of the bed and shrugged into it as he stumbled to the door. Lieutenant Coronado and a deputy in uniform El had never seen before stood at the door.

"Good morning, Reverend. Sleep well?"

El nodded as he tried to collect his thoughts. What brought Coronado here at this time of day?

"We received a tip last night, Reverend." Coronado smiled, but his eyes did not. "Said you were the drugmaker for Leroy. Are you?"

Coronado's words flushed the last remnants of sleep away, but all El could do was shake his head. He remembered his anonymous caller, so sure El made Leroy's drugs. *Had the same man called Coronado? Why?*

Coronado continued, "I have a warrant to search your home. Sorry, Reverend."

El shrugged. That didn't worry him. He unlocked the screen. "Come in."

Coronado and his man stepped past him. Coronado paused in the middle of the living room and looked around. Without a word the deputy began to search. Coronado watched him, but did nothing.

"Can I get dressed?" El asked.

Coronado blinked and looked at El as if he were just seeing him. "Sure. Right after we check your bedroom." He nodded to his deputy.

The deputy turned to El. "Where?"

El pointed to his bedroom. The deputy headed for it. Coronado did not move. Coronado said nothing to El while the deputy searched. El tried not to fidget, to seem calm.

When the deputy came out of El's bedroom, he shook his head and said, "It's clean."

"Good," Coronado replied. He turned to El. "You can get dressed."

"Thanks," El said with what he hoped was the right sarcastic tone.

As El dressed, he listened to the activity in the other part of the cabin. Obviously, from the sounds, the lieutenant had joined in the search.

After he dressed, he returned to the living room. Coronado was there alone.

"Can I shave?" El asked.

Coronado nodded. "Go ahead. We're through with the bathroom."

Once shaved, El went back in his living room. No one was there. He dropped into his easy chair, picked up the TV remote control and switched on the television. After changing channels several times, he switched it off. There was nothing worth watching. He sat. His mind skipped aimlessly from one thought to another.

Coronado came in, his face a mask. In his hand was a glass condenser.

El looked at it and grew cold all over. That condenser was from his college days. He'd forgotten that he had that old chemistry glassware in the storeroom downstairs, glassware that could be used for synthesizing drugs.

Coronado held it out. "We found a box of this stuff. What are you doing with it?"

El took a deep breath. "Look, I've had that since my undergraduate days at UT. When you break a piece of glassware in the lab you have to buy it. See, the end has been broken."

Coronado looked at the offending end. "Looks usable to me."

"It is," El said hastily. "That's why I kept it. My organic chemistry lab instructor was a real stickler for the rules. Even if you only chipped a piece, you had to buy it. That's how I got most of that in the box. After college I just never threw it away."

"Moved it with you, huh?"

El nodded. "I'm something of a pack rat."

The deputy appeared at the front door with the cardboard box of glassware. Coronado nodded at him. "Take it to the car. We're going to run a few tests on it, Reverend."

El nodded. Had Coronado emphasized "Reverend" a little too much?

"I'd like you to come down to the office with me."

El swallowed. "Am I under arrest?" El wondered if he should even ask that question. *On TV they always read you your rights before arresting you. Did they do that in Texas?*

"No, not yet. I would like you to come with me though."

"All right. Can I call the church first?"

Coronado nodded.

Much to his surprise, El dialed with a steady hand. Martha answered.

"Martha, this is Pastor El. Lieutenant Coronado dropped by my cabin this morning. He's here now. Things are getting a little complicated, so he wants me to go to his office with him this morning to straighten things out."

"Oh," Martha replied. "There's nothing wrong?"

"No, it's just routine, he says. Tell Steve where I am. I'll be in when I get through." El hoped that was true.

"Okay." There was a slight tremor in Martha's voice. "Good-bye."

"Good-bye." *I've upset her,* El thought. Well, there was nothing else he could have done.

The ride into town was silent. The deputy drove and Coronado sat beside El. Once at the sheriff's office, El was put in a small room with only a wooden table and three wooden chairs. It was an ugly room with no windows. The walls had been off-white originally, El guessed. Now they were a dingy yellow-gray. The floor was concrete. The ceiling was acoustic tile with two inset fluorescent fixtures and some kind of small vent near one wall. A couple of the the tiles sagged in their frames, the stains on them showed something had leaked. El wondered if it were rainwater or something else. The old jail was on the upper floor. Sometimes inmates stopped up the plumbing. That was not a pleasant thought. El glanced at his watch. He'd been in the room fifteen minutes.

Time passed. El tried to think about the week ahead, what needed to be done at church, but all he could do was wonder if he'd be arrested for Leroy's murder.

Just as El noted that an hour had passed, Coronado came in without knocking. "Good news, Reverend. We've done a preliminary check on that glassware and so far it's clean."

El tried to scowl. "Of course it was. I've done nothing."

"Probably not," Coronado agreed. "Course, you could've cleaned it up before you brought it home. You're smart enough to do that. Would you mind if we ran a urine test on you?"

El blinked. "No, I guess not." He wondered what would have happened if he objected. Would Coronado arrest him?

"Good," Coronado said. He opened the door and spoke to someone outside. "This officer will go with you." He held the door open wider.

El was relieved to see the officer was a man. You never knew these days. He followed him dutifully.

The officer guided him into a dingy bathroom and handed him a small container. "Fill it."

El started to turn away. The officer shook his head. "Where I can see."

El nodded and did it.

Five minutes later, he was back in the same room. Alone, again.

El tried to plan the Wednesday night service. He couldn't concentrate.

There was a knock on the door. El wondered why. Coronado hadn't bothered before.

"Come in," El said.

Steve Forbes walked in hesitantly. "Hi there."

"What are you doing here?" El asked.

"I heard you were arrested, so I thought I'd better come down and help. What are the charges?"

El shook his head. "I haven't been arrested. Did Martha tell you that?"

Steve looked at little sheepish. "No, Wayne McCarty called me at home. He told me you had been arrested for Leroy's murder."

El felt as if he stood on a precipice with a crumbling edge. His legs felt weak, even though he was sitting down.

"I see," El said, although that was not at all true.

"Listen," Steve said. "It was just a mistake. You can call him up when you get back to the office. Can you go soon?"

"I don't know, but I think you better call Brother McCarty. He might not believe me."

Steve frowned, "Okay, but maybe I should wait." He shifted from one foot to another awkwardly.

El knew from past experience that meant Steve had something more to say, but was unsure how El would react. "What is it, Steve?"

"I've got the name of a good lawyer for you. But you don't need it now," he added hastily.

"Well, why don't you give me the guy's name, so I'll have it just in case."

Steve fumbled in his jacket pocket for a moment then pulled out a piece of folded paper. "Here."

El took the paper and put it in his pocket. "Now go on back to the church. I'll be along soon."

Steve nodded and turned to go. Lieutenant Coronado stood blocking the door.

"Hello, Reverend Forbes, good to see you here."

Steve bobbed his head. "Yes, I mean . . ."

"Steve came down to spring me. He understood I'd been arrested." El tried to keep his voice calm. Coronado might still intend to make that arrest.

Coronado smiled. "Of course not. We just thought that Reverend Littlejohn might recall something pertinent if we could question him without distractions. Bringing him here was for our convenience."

El almost said "Bless you" at the lieutenant's words, but he restrained himself.

Coronado continued. "We're almost through. He'll be out of here before lunch."

Steve smiled, but El saw strain lines. "Okay. See you, El." He left.

Coronado turned his full attention to El. "Now let's go over Sunday a week ago."

The next hour was spent in grueling detail. Coronado went over the same facts again and again. When he finished, El felt wrung out.

"You've been a great help, Reverend. We'll be in touch. One of my men will drive you home."

El nodded and rose stiffly. The taciturn deputy that had driven him to the police station reappeared. He beckoned to El and El followed.

The ride back to his cabin was his first opportunity to contemplate what Steve had said. *Wayne McCarty would have told everyone he could about my arrest. The whole church probably knew by now. Where had McCarty gotten his information? From his friend in the district attorney's office? Did that mean that I am to be arrested at a later time? If so, why wait?*

When El got home, he spent only a few minutes there before he headed for the church. He would have liked a shower, but he figured he better get to the office. Martha was overjoyed to see him, and to El's surprise asked him no questions. El went into his office and closed the door.

He better make some calls. If he got his story out first, then maybe he could head off any trouble. First, Alice Taylor. He dialed her number and waited. No one answered. Sister Alice was not one to use an answering machine. El would have to try her later.

Next, he called Otis Wheeler at his office. Otis worked for the Highway Department. It took a moment to reach him, then he was on the line.

"What's the problem, Pastor?"

"I had a visit with Lieutenant Coronado at his office this morning. Somehow, Brother Wayne was told that I'd been arrested. I hadn't. I just wanted you to know."

"I understand, Pastor."

El waited for Otis to go on. He didn't, so El went on.

"There may be trouble at the next deacon's meeting over this. I wanted to know I could count on you."

"You don't have to worry, Pastor. I'm always on your side. I'll do my best to help you."

"Thanks, Brother Otis, I knew I could count on you."

"Keep me informed," Otis said.

"I will, good-bye." El hung up.

El called Henry Wieland. He had much the same conversation as with Otis until the end.

"Pastor, I'm real glad you told me what happened. Bill Gunter had called earlier. He told me you had been arrested. He was ready to ask you to resign."

El started to say something, but Henry cut him off. "Just listen, Pastor. I told him the church should stand by you. That we didn't want to be seen as dumping you. He agreed, so just sit tight. I'll call him and tell him he blew it. Let me handle it."

"Okay," El said.

El made a few more calls to shore up his support. None of the others he reached had heard anything before he called. They were all supportive. El only hoped he had enough people behind him to head off Gunter if it came to that.

El sat back in his chair and glanced around his office. A file cabinet sat against one wall, and El stared at it. All the information on individual church members was in the top drawer. He got up and went over to the file cabinet and pulled out the folder labeled A-C.

El sat down and opened the folder on his desk. He flipped through the sheets of paper until he came to one labeled Leroy Boyd. He pulled out that sheet. The church kept records on each of its members. Some of it was normal statistics: date of birth, where baptized, married, and so on. Other information had been added by the last minister, Marvin Thornhill. These notes outlined any particular problems the person's family had, talents, and any other observations Reverend Thornhill had made, a unique practice as far as El knew.

El had skimmed these files when he first came to Hill Country, but had never really studied them. He liked to make his own judgments about people. *Bad as they seemed to be,* he added to himself.

Leroy's page was remarkably empty for a long-standing member. It gave Leroy's date of birth, 2/19/42. *Leroy had seemed younger,* El thought just as he had at Leroy's funeral. El read on. Leroy graduated from Austin High School in 1960. A hometown boy, just like El. The file said some college, but did not list which one attended. Then there was family information, all familiar to El.

Now for the handwritten notes. The Reverend Marvin Thornhill had been in his seventies when he died, still the pastor. He had suffered a heart attack in this office. His handwriting was a tight, barely legible cursive. El had to admit that was one reason he had only scanned his notes.

Now, he tried to decipher the three lines at the bottom of the page. The first line was easy. "Generous giver, dependable. Likes to have his giving acknowledged."

El nodded to himself, very true. The old pastor had probably been a better judge of character than El.

"Leroy doing good job as treasurer."

El agreed. Leroy had done a good job as treasurer, too good. All that money. El read the last note by Thornhill.

"Leroy donated money for fellowship hall remodeling. Anonymously."

El shook his head. Had that money come from drugs? There was no way to know.

El laid Leroy's sheet to one side. He turned to the front of the file. He was going to read every one of these. If someone in the church was involved with Leroy maybe there was a clue to their identity in these files. At least, going over the file would make El think about each member and take his mind off his own troubles.

El started to read.

▲11▼

▛▀ L LEFT HIS office at six o' clock. He had tried to
reach Alice Taylor again, but she still wasn't
home. He wondered where she was, then had turned
back to the files. He'd only made it to the G-Is. He
decided to take some of the files home with him. No
one in the first group he had looked through seemed a
likely candidate for drug chemist. Maybe he was wrong,
maybe it wasn't anyone in the congregation. Maybe.
There had been some benefit from his reading. El had
learned more about members of his congregation, and
he was even more impressed with his predecessor.

"I should have read those files long ago, Lord," he
said as he drove home. "Most of the mistakes I've made
could have been prevented. Was it my own ego that kept
me from it? Lord, you sure have a poor servant here,
and I don't mean money poor, but of course, you know
that. Rambling aren't I, Lord? Have you any sugges-
tions, Lord?"

As usual, El received no divine revelation.

After supper, El started through the membership files
again. He'd been at it for about forty-five minutes when
the phone rang. El answered it.

"Hello, Reverend."

The voice chilled El. It was Leroy's accomplice, the
voice disguised as before.

"What do you want?" El tried to keep the anger out of his voice.

"Reverend, I want to confess."

"Confess to what?"

"I know who killed Leroy, Reverend. I want to talk to you about it."

"All right."

"Not over the phone. Can you meet me at church?"

"If you tell me who you are."

"I can't tell you that yet, Reverend. They might have your phone bugged."

"Who's they?" El had not thought of the possibility that someone would bug his phone.

"Sheriff, some of your friends. You never know."

"I see. When do you want to meet?"

"How about right now? I'll meet you at the church."

"All right."

"No sheriff."

"No sheriff," El repeated.

The caller hung up. Was the man telling the truth? Did he know who killed Leroy? El looked at the phone. He should tell Coronado no matter what the caller said. El shook his head. No. He was a minister. He'd meet the man. What if the man wanted to hurt him? Again, El shook his head. This cabin was pretty isolated. If someone was after him, this place made it easy.

Fifteen minutes later, El pulled into the church parking lot. There were no other cars. He waited.

El glanced at his watch. He'd been sitting here twenty minutes. He climbed out of his car and walked around. He checked the doors on the church office and the sanctuary, all locked. He did not open them. El returned to the church office, but did not go in, instead he leaned against the railing and waited. A cricket chirped somewhere nearby. A half hour later, El knew no one was going to show up. He started home. Had this all been a practical joke?

As he turned the Mustang onto the subdivision road, a car came up behind his. It stayed on his tail. Annoyed, El speeded up. The car dropped back. Suddenly, another car pulled out of a driveway in front of him. El slammed on his brakes and swung his car to the right. His car stopped inches from the other. Behind him that other car pulled up and stopped. El's grip on the steering wheel tightened. His heart pounded. Were these guys after him?

Yes. One man got out of the car ahead. He had a gun in his hand and a stocking over his head.

Could he make a run for it on foot in the dark? A second stocking-headed man was at El's car door. El glanced toward the passenger side. Still another stocking masked figure crouched there. The man at El's window, tapped on it with a gun. El rolled down the window.

"Get out slow, minister. Real slow," the man said.

El got out. There were three men, all in the same stocking masks, all in dark pants and shirts. One was tall and thin, the other average height and build, while the third was much shorter. "Shorty" was giving the orders.

"Get in the car." He indicated the vehicle in front with his gun. Its left rear door was open.

El did as he was told. In the dark, he couldn't tell if the car was dark blue or black. Once inside, he realized this was an expensive car. The seats looked like gray leather, and the carpet was plush. El took a deep breath to calm himself. His heart was beating so hard, he almost expected the men to hear it. What were they going to do with him?

Shorty slid in beside him. "Turn around. Hands behind you."

El faced away from him. The man grabbed El's wrists roughly and fastened them together with some stiff material. Then, he put a blindfold over El's eyes.

El heard the front door of the car open, then close. Shorty's door closed. The car started.

"Where are you taking me? Why?" El asked.

"Shut up," Shorty said and punched El in the side with what El assumed was the barrel of his gun.

El said nothing more. Why had they bothered to get him away from his cabin? They could have kidnapped him from there with no problem. Why send him on the wild-goose chase to the church? El couldn't figure it out. He decided to concentrate on listening to the sounds of the road. Maybe he could figure out where they were or where they were going. The car was still on a gravel road. They turned and stopped. After a few minutes, the left front door opened.

"I parked it," the newcomer said. He slammed the door.

The car turned around. Back the way it had come? El was not sure if the car had turned completely. They were on gravel. After some time the gravel changed to pavement, then they turned right still on pavement. If they had taken the same road back, they were on Highway 71 now.

El was sure he was correct because the car accelerated. More time passed. They turned right off the highway. The ride was smooth with only occasional bumps. Paved roads, but not as well-maintained as the highway, El decided. There followed a number of twists and turns until El lost track. Once he was sure they were back on the highway, but only for a short distance.

El heard a *whump* as they crossed a cattle guard, a few seconds passed, then a *whump* again. Two in a row. Strange. The car traveled a ways on pavement, then turned onto gravel or maybe dirt. The car stopped. Doors opened.

Shorty spoke. "Get out, Preacher."

El scooted awkwardly across the seat toward the sound of Shorty's voice. He tried to feel for the edge of the seat with his hands. He pictured himself falling out of the car, but a hand grabbed his upper arm, dragged him out and up. El almost fell as he got his feet under him, but the man holding his arm, steadied him.

"Come on," a man said. El couldn't identify the voice.

Someone poked El in the back. El stumbled forward. This was awful, walking in darkness like this. His heart thudded. What were these men going to do? Shoot him? Behind him, someone muttered unintelligibly. Suddenly, El was grabbed by each arm and marched forward at a quick pace.

"Steps, three of 'em," the man on El's right said. At the same time he lifted up on El's arm. El made the first two steps but missed the third. Only the men on either side kept him from falling.

A door opened. El felt the cool of air conditioning. The men urged him forward into the coolness. The door closed behind him.

"Take him into the living room," a voice El thought was new said. The voice seemed tantalizingly familiar.

The two men marched El to the right, then pushed him into what must be an overstuffed chair. El sank down gratefully. He tried to relax, but his upper arms were beginning to ache.

"Okay, take off his blindfold." It was the new voice again.

Someone jerked El's blindfold off. He blinked in a bright light shining straight into his face. He could only see dark silhouettes behind it. His eyes watered and even the silhouettes were hard to make out. He wished his hands were free so he could block that light out of his face.

"We need some information, Preacher, and we need that last batch of stuff you made for Leroy. It wasn't in your cabin." The man speaking stood directly behind the light.

So they had searched his cabin. Maybe they hadn't planned to kidnap him originally. El shook his head. How could he make these men believe him?

"I don't know anything, and I never made any stuff for Leroy. If he told you that, he lied."

"I see," said the man behind the light. "I don't have time to waste."

El saw him jerk his head toward another silhouette. The light went out. El could see nothing. Hands grabbed his arm and pushed back his sleeve. El struggled. He had heard too many stories of people becoming addicted from only one injection. *Dear Lord, I don't want to be a drug addict!*

"I told you the truth. I don't know anything about drugs. You don't have to do this."

El felt the sharp stab of the needle, then it was gone. There was no rush of drug induced euphoria, no pleasure sensation, only a kind of spreading lassitude.

"Don't worry, Preacher. We're just going to make sure you're telling the truth. The drug we gave you is something pretty new and real good. You'll tell us the truth."

As the man spoke, his dark outline seemed to float closer. The light grew less intense. Again, El felt that he'd heard the voice before. He said something El couldn't hear. The wall in front of El changed. Someone had opened the curtains. El felt proud of himself for figuring that out. They were near a lake. El saw boat lights and their reflections on the water. The lights grew larger and dimmer. El tried to clear his head, he couldn't. A man was next to him, but El couldn't see his face. The room was getting hazy. Voices. *Who was talking so much?*

El woke slowly. What a nightmare. He stretched and banged his hands against a wall. He was not in his bed. He sat up. Where was he? The room was totally dark.

No. There was a sliver of light about six feet away at floor level. El started to get up. His hands slid over the slick surface around him. A bathtub, he was in a bathtub. He pulled himself up on the edge of the tub and put his legs on the floor. He did not stand up. There seemed to be no ill effects from last night. Last night? What time was it?

If this was a bathroom, then there should be a light. He stood stiffly and shuffled toward the sliver of light. Yes, there was a door. El tried the knob; locked, of course. He slid his hand around the wall next to the knob. He was rewarded by the light switch. He flipped it on. Light flooded the room.

El blinked rapidly. His eyes watered, then cleared. He was in an ordinary looking bathroom. White birds on a silvery blue background decorated the upper walls while the lower part of the wall was white tile. Even the floor was white tile. This room must be hell to keep clean, but someone sure did clean it. Even the grout was still white.

One immaculate, white towel hung on the rack next to the sink. There was a medicine cabinet above the sink. He opened it. Inside was a bottle of aspirin, some Band-Aids and a bottle of mouthwash. Nothing else. El closed the cabinet. He looked in the cabinet under the sink. Extra toilet paper.

He went back to the door. He tried the knob again. No luck. Bathroom locks were not very sturdy, maybe he could force this one. He shoved. Nothing. He drew back and threw himself against the door. The lock held, and from the other side came an angry voice.

"Try that again, Preacher, and I'll come in there and tie you up."

El did not reply. He retreated to the only seat in the room and sat down on the toilet. The tank and seat were covered with a white polyester tank set. El ran his fingers over it as he tried to recall last night after the injection. It was a blur. Those voices. Abruptly, El realized one of those voices had been his, but he did not remember what he had said.

El looked at his watch. Five o'clock. Morning or afternoon? He had no way of knowing. Probably afternoon, El decided as he became aware of how hungry he was. Should he ask for food? No. He wouldn't give them the satisfaction of knowing how hungry he felt. He'd just wait.

The time passed slowly. El paced some, but six feet was hardly room for more than a couple of steps. He drank some water. Did it taste different than his? His cabin was on Austin water. He drank some more. This, he was sure, was not Austin water. He remembered the boat lights. He must be somewhere near Lake Travis.

Lord, what is going to happen? Are these men going to kill me?

Not likely since they hadn't already. Why hadn't they turned him loose once they knew he wasn't the drugmaker?

Sorry, Lord, lost my train of thought. I was talking to you, Lord. Give me strength, Oh Lord, give me strength, Amen. El began to recite the 23rd Psalm. "The Lord is my shepherd . . ."

▲12▼

EL LOOKED AT his watch. He tried not to, but it was a compulsion. Nine-thirty. If he were right about the time of day, it would be dark now. His hunger had actually subsided, although, if he thought about it, the discomfort returned.

The doorknob rattled. El stood up. Two men with stocking masks entered. The taller wore a black sweatsuit, while the other, "Shorty," wore gray pants and a black, long-sleeve shirt.

"You're coming with us, Preacher," Shorty said.

El shrugged. Both men had guns, there was no use arguing. At least this time, they did not tie his hands or blindfold him. The lights were out in the rest of the house, but to his left he caught a glimpse of a living room furnished in, he thought, blue and white before they hustled him out. He almost lost his footing as he stepped out the door so intent was he on that room. He looked down to keep from falling and saw no more of the house interior. The door slammed behind them.

Outside, not even the front steps were lighted. It was so dark that El felt like he was walking off a cliff, stepping into space. Somehow, he stumbled down the steps. The taller man caught El's arm to steady him. El bit back thanks. You didn't thank your kidnapper.

El's eyes were adjusting to the darkness. He could

just make out the outline of a van. The two men roughly guided him to the back of it. El could not tell its color, only that it was dark. They pushed him inside.

"Sit down," Shorty indicated a cardboard box.

El sat. The box must be reinforced, El thought, since it supported El with no give. Shorty climbed in behind him and sat on another box across from El. He still held a gun. The other man climbed in the front. El's nose twitched. The van had a decidedly chemical odor, like the old chemistry building on campus.

"Where are you taking me?" El asked. He didn't expect an answer.

To his surprise, Shorty answered. "You're going to cook us up some stuff. We got a spot out in the boonies just right for that, where no one will bother us. Even got a generator." The man tapped a plastic-covered object on El's left with his foot.

The van lurched forward giving El a moment to gather his thoughts for a reply. "I told you I'm not your supplier."

Shorty nodded. "We know. That drug last night worked real good. You told us everything."

El's stomach knotted. What had he revealed?

The other continued. "You're a chemist. That's what we need right now. Leroy's old clients are getting pretty strung out. So you'll brew us up a batch to keep them happy."

"I can't. I don't know how."

"It's okay. We've got a recipe. It may not be as good as our regular stuff, but it'll do. Don't think you can try any funny stuff either. I know a little about making it."

"Exactly what will I be making?"

"Alpha methylfentanyl."

"Oh." El tried to remember the structure of fentanyl. He had no luck. He should have looked it up when the deputy first mentioned it.

El noticed that the van was slowing. There was a

bump, and El grabbed the sides of the box to keep his seat, his hands slid into holes cut in the sides for handles. He held on for a moment, then relaxed and brought his hands back to his lap. The ride was smoother now. El guessed they had pulled onto the highway.

The van had no windows in its sides or the back. All El could get was occasional glimpses out the front. In the dark, he could see little.

El looked at Shorty. The man had leaned back against the side of the van, completely relaxed. His gun was held loosely in his hand, which rested on his leg. El stared at the box Shorty sat on. An oncoming vehicle's lights briefly lit the van's interior. Nitric acid. El gulped and looked down at his own seat. The interior lit again. Another box of nitric. He waited for more passing cars. Each time their lights swept the van, he studied the label of another container.

By the time they pulled off the highway onto a rougher road, El knew the entire contents of the van. Now, he was just as afraid to be riding in it as of getting shot. Some of these chemicals were highly explosive. On his right sat four bottles of methyl acrylate in a Styrofoam crate. El would hate to be around that if some of that spilled. Methyl acrylate irritated the eyes and nose, it would be as bad as tear gas. Worse, if he remembered correctly, in high concentrations, it brought on convulsions.

El had a thought. *If a bottle of methyl acrylate spilled, it would incapacitate anyone around. Including himself. But if he were prepared and they weren't? Maybe.*

El coughed. Shorty didn't move. El couldn't tell if he was asleep or not. El leaned back against the side of the van and let his right hand slide off his lap. Shorty still didn't move. El touched a bottle of methyl acrylate, but he never took his eyes off Shorty. He ran his fingers around the top, then grasped the cap with his thumb and first two fingers. He twisted. The cap did not move.

Shorty shifted. El let his hand drop to his side. Shorty settled down again. El slowly raised his hand back to the bottle. He tried the cap again. This time it turned. Carefully, El unscrewed the cap one half turn at a time. Suddenly, he caught a whiff of methyl acrylate. His nose twitched at the acrid odor. He quickly twisted the cap the rest of the way off. Holding his breath, he grabbed the bottle by its handle and pulled it free of the Styrofoam. He swung it toward the driver and let go. It crashed against his seat.

Shorty woke up. Already the fumes were clawing at El's eyes. Shorty gasped and choked. El shoved him forward and pulled at the rear door. It wouldn't open. The van swung violently to one side. He heard the driver shout something. El clutched the door handle tighter. The van crashed, teetered, but did not roll over. El almost lost his grip on the door from the jolt, but he held on. If he had let go, he would have been thrown the length of the van. Shorty was. Shorty crumpled to the floor behind the driver. The bottom half of the bottle of methyl acrylate rolled to one side.

El let go of the back door and stumbled forward. He tried to stay as far away as he could from the broken jug. His eyes were watering so badly that he could barely see, and he was going to choke or vomit. Somehow, he climbed over the seat and out the door. He stumbled away from the van and stood gasping and crying. He stared blearily at the van. Should he pull his captors out? Through his tears he saw the driver stagger out. El realized his danger. Shorty and his companion were armed. He'd better get out of here.

He ran back down the road, but every fifty yards or so he had to stop and retch. He had no plan. Just put as much distance between himself and the van as possible. He kept going. He couldn't stay on the road much longer, his kidnappers could see him too easily if they gave chase.

Up ahead, he saw an area of darkness off the north side of the road, and he turned into it. It was a ravine of some sort. El hoped it went back a ways. Clumps of grass gave way to heavier brush. El slowed down. There was some light, but his eyes were still watering. He could hurt himself badly if he were not careful. Plenty of these ravines ended in sharp drop-offs to limestone shelves.

He wasn't sure how far he had come when he saw a rocky outcrop about five feet above his head. If it was wide enough, he could hide on it and not be seen from below. He climbed toward it. He was lucky. There was a shallow cave behind it. Gratefully, he climbed into it and huddled against the back wall.

Maybe he should keep running, but his body told him the answer. Every breath was loud and wheezy, and his legs ached. He was not used to exercise, especially after not eating for a day. He'd take his chances here. In the morning, if they hadn't found him, he'd make his way back to the road.

El didn't expect to sleep. He did need to do one thing though. "Dear Lord, thank you for giving me a chance to escape. Keep me safe this night. Amen."

El's foot was hot. He moved it out of the sun. *Out of the sun.* El came fully awake with all of yesterday's events flooding his mind. He looked around. A limestone wall arched over him. About ten feet away and directly across from him, a scraggly cedar clung tenaciously to a small ledge on a similar wall. El looked back the way he had come. The ravine was choked with brush. How had he made it through in the dark? Well, if he could do it in the dark, he could do it in daylight. He looked at his watch. Seven o'clock.

He tried to move and found that every muscle in his body was stiff and sore. His back felt as if someone were sticking a dull knife in it. His head didn't feel so good either. He couldn't remember if methyl acrylate had any long-term effects. He hoped not.

El flexed his legs. His bad knee complained, but seemed surprisingly limber. Gingerly, he climbed down from his perch.

Once he reached the bottom of the ravine, he could see the brush was not as thick as it had looked from above. He looked back at his ledge. Another thought made his heart beat quicken. *This is rattlesnake country.* Last night, he could have crawled into a den of snakes.

"Thank you, Lord, for keeping me safe."

El picked his way back toward the road, careful to dodge the worst of the thorny chaparral and mesquite. He'd done better last night than he'd realized. If he had fallen into one of those chapparal . . . El shuddered at the thought.

Ten minutes later, concealed behind a cedar, he watched a car kick up clouds of dust as it sped down the dirt road. Would his kidnappers be looking for him? He'd have to chance it. The road was the only way to safety. He had no idea where he was.

Soon, he was trudging down the road. He chose to go in the direction opposite from where he had left the wrecked van. He walked for about ten minutes before a pickup approached from behind. He willed himself not to run into the nearby brush. The truck stopped.

El looked at the driver and relaxed. The driver was an old man in striped shirt and worn overalls with a stained, straw hat on his head. His deeply lined face said he'd seen a lot of Texas summers. El doubted that this old man was a member of a drug ring.

"You need a ride, son?" said the old man.

"I sure do. My buddy and I had a fight, and he dumped me." El did not see any need to tell this man about what really happened. Besides, the old man would probably think he was crazy.

"I'm going to Bee Caves," the old man said. "Name is George Neeley."

"Mine's Lee, John Lee." *Why did I lie to the man,* El wondered. "Bee Caves would be great. You can drop me at a subdivision just before there."

The old man nodded. El climbed in. It was a relief to sit down. The pickup groaned into gear, and they bounced off. It was not until they reached the highway that El knew where he was, about five miles from Bee Caves.

A siren wailed in the distance. Coming their way.

The old man muttered to himself. "Damn lot of noise."

A highway patrol car, the wailing's source, slowed as it approached their road. The old man pulled to his side of the road, giving the patrol car plenty of room. The patrolman touched his hat to the old man as he sped by.

El watched the vehicle as the old man turned on to the highway. "I wonder where he is going?" El said, more to himself than his companion.

"Probably going to look at that wrecked van."

"Wrecked van?" El hoped he kept his voice calm.

"Yep, I passed it a ways before I met you. Thought at first it might be yours."

El shook his head. "No way. No one with it?"

The old man shook his head. "Nope. Looked like some fella had too much to drink and just ran her off the road." The old man squinted at El.

He probably thinks I'm the one, El decided.

Nothing more was said until they reached the subdivision entrance.

"I can drive you home, if you want. You look pretty done in," George Neeley said.

The offer took El by surprise, but he shook his head. "Thanks, I can make it from here." He didn't want the old man to know exactly where he lived.

He climbed out. His body reminded him of how last

night was spent. He waved as the old man drove off, then started for home. A half mile down the road, he regretted turning down Neeley's offer. Twenty minutes later, he saw his cabin. His car was there. He stopped, surprised, then he remembered the stop his kidnappers made after they picked him up. One of them must have driven it here.

El fumbled in his pocket for his keys. At least he still had them. That was one good thing. The kidnappers hadn't even searched him. He opened his front door and stepped inside. The air conditioner was still on. He glanced around. Evidence of his kidnappers' search was everywhere. His chairs were out of place and while some of his books were stacked on the floor, others were scattered across the room. Well, he'd worry about that later. A minute later, El thirstily gulped down a glass of milk. The kitchen did not appear disturbed. He poured another glass of milk and looked in the freezer for some food. There was a TV breakfast. In minutes, El was sitting down to a hot meal.

When he finished, he thought for the first time about his situation. What should he do? Two weeks ago, he'd have called the sheriff without another thought. Now, he wondered if he should. Would it just throw more suspicion on him?

El sighed. It didn't matter, the right thing to do was report it. "Right, Lord?"

Five minutes later, El finished telling Lieutenant Coronado the highlights of the last thirty-six hours. Coronado had not interrupted him.

"Well, Reverend, I think I better come out to see you so I can get the details. Unless you'd like to come here?"

"No, I'd rather not." El was surprised Coronado had not insisted.

"Okay, I'll be at your place in half an hour."

After he hung up, El checked the time. Eight-thirty.

He'd better call the office. While he dialed, he rehearsed what he would say. Martha answered.

"Martha, this is Pastor El." El heard her take a quick breath. "Stay calm. I'm fine, but I'm going to be late coming in."

"Oh, Pastor, I'm so glad you're all right. When you didn't come in yesterday we were so worried. Steve went to your house, but you weren't there. He called the sheriff, but no one knew what had happened."

"That's all right, Martha. I'll explain when I get in, but I won't be in until after lunch. Good-bye." El hung up before Martha could reply.

So, Steve had told the sheriff he was missing. Had the sheriff known what happened? Maybe Coronado would tell him.

El called his parents. His dad should have gotten in Sunday night. They must have been told he was missing.

His mother answered. "Oh, El. Are you okay? We were so worried. Let me tell your father."

El heard his mother call to his father. "It's El, he's all right."

"El, are you there?" she asked.

"Yes, mom. I'm here."

"A deputy sheriff came by and asked about you, told us you were missing. He asked the strangest questions."

"I'm fine. I just had an adventure. I'll tell you both about it over a supper next week. I don't have time now. Okay?"

"You're sure you're all right? We can come over. Your Dad took some time off."

"I'm sure, Mother. Tell Dad hello."

"Of course. Take care."

"I love."

"I love."

Coronado arrived precisely at nine. El was not sure, but he thought the investigator's eyes were less unfriendly than the last time they met. El repeated what he had told him over the phone, but with more detail. Coronado interrupted now and then to ask a question, but mostly he let El tell his story his own way. He did ask about the mess the cabin was in. It had been like this when El's parents let a deputy in to look around. El assured him that this was the work of his kidnappers, not his housekeeping. Coronado nodded.

"That's what I thought when I first heard about it. When we searched, your place was pretty neat. I figure when they didn't find what they wanted here, they kidnapped you. When it turned out you didn't have their missing batch, they wanted you to cook up some. Synthetic heroin is something new in these parts. Lots of the real stuff and crack, but not synthetic. Did they tell you where they were taking you?" Coronado asked.

"No, but I had the feeling it was just some camp in back in the cedar. They had everything they needed in the van including a generator."

"That's true. I got a report on that van before I left." Coronado chuckled.

El realized that was the first time he had heard the man laugh.

"What's so funny?" El asked.

"You did a job on that van. Our men had to go in with gas masks to examine it. That methyl acrylate must have soaked in. No one can get closer than a foot without crying. No wonder those guys didn't catch you." Coronado's black eyes found El's, there was no humor in them.

"You be careful, Reverend. These guys are bad news, and there's lots of money involved." Coronado paused, then continued. "But, I don't think they'll come after you again."

"I'm glad you think so," El said. He wished he felt so confident that he had seen the last of those men. "Do you think you can find the house where I was held?"

"You didn't give us much to go on, but we'll try."

"Maybe we could drive around. I think I could recognize the place from the outside, and I'd know that bathroom for sure."

"That's a long shot, Reverend, but I'll keep it in mind. We can't just walk in to check bathrooms. Besides, we've got some other leads for now. You take it easy." Coronado stood, nodded, and left.

El frowned at the man's back. Why wouldn't he let El try? El shook his head. He'd better bathe and change. He'd told Martha he'd be in today. Not the brightest thing to do.

▲13▼

As El pulled into the church parking lot, he checked for cars he didn't recognize. Only Martha's Olds and Steve's Honda sat in the baking sun. El relaxed a little as he guided his Mustang in beside the Honda. He stood next to his car for a moment after he got out. Why had he thought the place would be different? He'd only been absent one day. But enough musing, he had work to do. He headed toward the office.

The sound of a motor stopped him. *Was it the sheriff again?* He glanced back. It was Harry in his old pickup. That truck was not only old, it was ugly. El had never decided what its original color had been since each fender sported a different hue, and the hood didn't match any of them. The rest of the truck had a uniform coat of rust, so the mystery of the original color seemed unsolvable. Not that the color mattered to Harry, he'd told El more than once that the truck was a bit ugly, but it got him where he wanted to go. El sometimes wondered how.

Harry waved at El. He pulled the pickup over to the corner of the parking lot and stopped. El smiled. Harry always parked the truck there. Maybe he thought the pickup wasn't an appropriate vehicle to be parked in front of a church office. Harry hurried toward him. His jeans were cinched tight at his waist and his light blue shirt neatly tucked in. The way he moved belied his seventy years.

"Mr. El, Mr. El, you're okay?"

"I'm fine, Harry. Just had a little adventure."

"I'm mighty glad to hear that, Mr. El. I need to talk to you."

"What is it, Harry?" Harry's face was more deeply furrowed than usual. *What was the old man worrying about?*

"Mr. El, there's something you should know."

"Okay, let's go into my office." The August heat was getting to El.

Harry shook his head. "Nope, I'd rather talk in the church."

"There's no one in the office but Martha and Steve. Besides we'd be in my office."

Harry's expression hardened. El had seen that flinty look in those rheumy eyes before. Harry would talk with him in the church or nowhere, El knew that from past experience.

"The church," El agreed.

He and Harry walked to the side door of the sanctuary in silence. *What was bothering the old man? Who did Harry not want to overhear his conversation? Steve? Martha?*

Harry got out his keys when they reached the building. El was surprised, the sanctuary was usually unlocked during the day. They only locked it at night and on Saturdays. Steve unlocked it each day. Harry was responsible for locking it each night.

"Why is the sanctuary locked?"

Harry scowled. "Mr. Steve told me to lock it up yesterday and to keep it locked unless I was in here cleaning or he would authorize someone else to be here."

"Oh." El wondered why Steve had done that. *Maybe, he was worried about curiosity seekers. Probably was a good idea.*

Once inside, El walked to the nearest pew and sat down. Harry shut the door and locked it, then he came over to El's pew, but he did not sit, even though El motioned him to.

"Mr. El, you know I've worked for this church for ten years. Before that for another church. In all that time, I never told anyone what I'm going to tell you." Harry nervously rubbed his hands against his coveralls.

"Harry, you don't have to tell me."

"No, I've got to. The sheriff may know already. If that Mr. Gunter finds out, he'll want me out, I betcha. But I'm going to tell you, and if you think I should quit, well, I will."

El could only nod. "Okay."

"I killed a man back in thirty-nine. He pressed me hard, Mr. El. Real hard. Finally, one day he jumped me when I was coming home from a job. I'd had enough, I tell you. So's I took my knife and killed him."

El could not think of what to say. He could not picture this old man as a killer. When Harry said nothing more, El prodded him. "What happened after that?"

"Oh, the judge said there was plenty of witness to how ornery this guy was, and how he had had it in for me for no good reason. The law didn't give me no trouble. Called it self-defense."

El relaxed. "Harry, if it was self-defense, then you did nothing wrong."

Harry shook his head. "It was a killing, and I meant to do it. I could have hurt the fellow real bad, but I wanted him dead, out of my way. I killed him for sure. I doubt your church folks would understand. I figure the sheriff already knows. He may think that I killed Mr. Boyd."

"I don't think you are a suspect, Harry. Right now, I think it's me."

Harry's eyes widened. "You're kidding, Mr. El. You couldn't kill no one. I can see it in your eyes."

"Thanks, Harry, but I don't think the sheriff sees that. Don't worry about your past, Harry. No one has to know. I won't tell anyone."

" 'Specially, that Steve Forbes, Mr. El."

"What's the matter with Steve?" El asked. He'd noticed before some tension between Harry and Steve.

"I don't trust him. He thinks I don't improve the image of this church. He'd like to get one of those high-falutin cleaning services and a landscaper to take care of the church. Cost twice as much as me."

"What gave you that idea?"

"I overheard him talking to Mr. Gunter about what this church needs. Wants to reach a more 'affluent population.' " Harry managed to mimic Steve perfectly.

El was not surprised that Steve had said that to Bill Gunter. It was one of the few things that he and Steve argued about. El wanted to reach those new, young families and middle-class retirees moving into the new subdivisions. Steve wanted to expand their ministry to reach the wealthy people building lake homes in the area. El would like to do both, but he believed by attracting one group, they probably excluded the other. Steve at first had insisted that both were possible, but in time he had come to agree with El that only one group could be reached. He wanted that group to be rich. El shook his head. That was unfair. Steve simply thought that the more affluent group would help the church grow faster.

Bill Gunter thought like Steve or was it vice versa. El knew that from past discussions with Brother Bill. Was that one of the reasons he opposed El so often? El had never before thought of that. That thought didn't make him feel very secure.

"Well, as long as I am pastor, Harry, you have a job."

"Thanks, Mr. El . I appreciate that. You watch your back now."

El nodded. He understood that Harry was not speaking in a literal sense. "I'll watch it."

Harry fixed El with his watery, blue eyes. "What did happen to you?"

El explained briefly. The old man grinned from ear to ear when El described his escape.

"Good going," Harry said. "Well, I'd better get to work. You take care, Mr. El." He winked conspiratorially at El.

El nodded, then watched as Harry unlocked the door and ambled out of the sanctuary. *What you didn't know about people.* As El walked toward the church office, he went over the conversation with Harry again. He hadn't known that Steve had talked to Bill Gunter about the demographics of the congregation. He didn't want to start distrusting Steve, but . . .

"Oh, Lord, help me. Take away my doubts. Help me through this time. I need your strength, Dear Lord. Amen."

El squared his shoulders and opened the door. Martha stood up. Her eyes filmed with tears.

"Oh, Pastor, I'm so glad to see you." She came around her desk and hugged him.

"I'm glad to see you," El said and patted her back.

Martha stepped away and dabbed her eyes with a tissue.

A door opened. Steve Forbes came out of his office. He rushed forward and hugged El, too.

"Thank God, you're okay. When you didn't turn up yesterday, we were really worried. What happened?"

El pulled away from Steve. Right now, he didn't want to be touched by the man. He did owe both Martha and Steve an explanation. Briefly, he again described his adventures since Monday evening. El wondered how many times he would repeat this tale. When he finished Steve looked at him in amazement.

"You got away from them on your own. Wow!"

"I was very lucky, and the Lord was with me."

"Amen to that," Steve agreed.

"Now, I need you to bring me up-to-date on what's been happening since Monday night," El said to Steve and guided him toward his office. El smiled at Martha as he closed the door. Her eyes were still wet.

Once in his office, El went to his desk and picked up his mail. He fingered through it quickly. Nothing. Steve dropped into the chair in front of his desk. El sat on the edge.

"Anything exciting?"

Steve shook his head. "No, if you don't call the pastor's disappearance exciting."

El smiled. "Okay, that was exciting. How'd you find out I was missing."

"Well," Steve said, "I came in about eight-thirty and was surprised you weren't here. I called your house, but all I got was your answering machine. When Martha told me you hadn't called in, I got a little worried, but I figured you were just running late.

"Sheriff's deputies came around here two or three times Tuesday morning. The last time, they'd been by your place. They didn't tell me for what. One of them told me you weren't home, but your car was. That was when I really got worried. I drove over to your cabin to check, but your front door was locked. I looked in the window. It looked like your stuff had been tossed around. I called that Lieutenant Coronado, and I think he got hold of your parents because later he told me that they had let him in. He said it looked as if your house had been searched. I was afraid you had been killed. You had us mighty scared."

"I was pretty scared myself," El agreed. "Many people know?"

"Just about the whole church. Different ones called yesterday, Martha told 'em you were missing. I figured that it was better to be honest."

El nodded. *Had Steve told him everything?* Was his conversation with Harry making El suspicious of Steve? There was no reason to be suspicious. Still . . .

Lord, I need you now, if I mistrust Steve, El thought.

Steve looked as if he was waiting for El's approval. He had that eager puppy-dog look that El could not resist.

"I appreciate all you did, Steve. Listen, I plan to spend the rest of the afternoon here, then go to church supper. Would you mind handling the service tonight?"

"I'll be glad to," Steve said. "I sort of planned to already."

"Good, then I'll get to work on this other stuff."

El stood as Steve did. He reached out and patted Steve's shoulder. "Thanks for taking over."

Steve nodded and left, closing the door behind him. El looked at the closed door. "God, I'm such a hypocrite. Thanking him when deep down I believe he's not telling me everything. He probably talked to Gunter plenty. Getting ready to take over my job, I bet. Sorry, Lord, I should be more trusting. Oh, Dear Lord, help."

El sat down at his desk. He started to look through his correspondence, but his phone rang. Otis Wheeler had called to find out any news, and Martha connected him with El directly. El reassured Brother Otis that he was just fine. El asked if he had heard anything from Bill Gunter, but Otis hadn't. El didn't know whether to be relieved or worried.

As soon as he hung up the phone rang again. Another worried member checking on their lost minister. The calls continued. El didn't have the heart to tell Martha not to connect them. Besides, she probably wouldn't have listened anyway. El had to admit he really didn't mind the attention, and he was surprised how many seemed genuinely concerned.

Alice Taylor called about mid-afternoon. "Oh, Pastor, I'm so glad you're safe."

"Me, too, Sister Taylor."

"Pastor, I need to talk to you about something, something very important."

El heard a tremor in her voice. She must be very close to tears. This was not the time to share his problems with her. "Of course, Sister Taylor. I tried to reach you the other day, myself. The rest of this week is pretty clear."

"Oh, I can't see you for a few days. I wish I could, but I've got house guests. They are leaving Sunday morning. I could visit with you Sunday afternoon. Would that be all right?"

"Of course. Right after church?"

"Yes."

"See you then."

After she hung up, El wondered what was bothering her, but he soon forgot her call as more inquisitive church members phoned to check on him. Henry Wieland called around four. He had tried to reach Bill Gunter and Wayne McCarty earlier and not been successful. He had no news for El.

El decided to stay in the office until suppertime. It was a relief not to be planning this evening's service. Around four-thirty, the calls finally stopped. He made himself tend to his correspondence and to bills that needed his immediate attention. He finished paying the last bill at five-fifteen, but waited until five-thirty to leave the office. Steve had left at five. El locked the office door behind him.

▲14▼

PEOPLE WERE ALREADY in line for supper when El entered Fellowship Hall. Everyone turned to look at him, then they all rushed over to greet him. El was stunned by the emotion of the group. Several of the men had tears in their eyes while the women wept openly. All asked about his absence yesterday. El described what had happened briefly. The eyes of his listeners widened as he talked. To his surprise, no one asked any questions. He thanked them and suggested that it was time to eat. They insisted he go through the line first. Tonight's supper was ham, sweet potatoes, a small lettuce salad, and spice cake. El sighed; he didn't like ham.

Wayne McCarty motioned to him. Wayne and his wife were seated at one of the front tables. They must have gotten their food before El arrived. El didn't want to talk to Wayne, but he knew there was really no choice. He smiled. *Hypocrite,* he said to himself. He walked over to Wayne's table and sat down across from him.

"How you doing, Pastor?" Wayne asked.

"Fine, Brother Wayne, just fine."

"I called earlier, and Martha told me about your adventures. You were awfully lucky."

Wayne said the last with apparent sincerity, but El

thought he detected a hint of sarcasm. *What did Wayne think? That he had made a deal with the drug dealers? Probably. Maybe he just thought that I was one of them already, that my adventure had just been a fight among criminals.* Mentally, El shook his head. That was too cynical.

"Yes I was lucky, but I prefer to think that God was helping a little."

"Of course, Pastor, of course."

The conversation drifted into mundane topics, weather and sports, to El's relief. He was not much of a baseball fan, but he kept up just for such occasions as this. In the fall, it was easier. He followed the Cowboys and the UT Longhorns. Church members didn't always understand if you didn't share their interests, especially if those interests were ones that most believed every man should have.

El finished eating just as Steve rose to start the evening service. Briefly, he explained to the congregation El's kidnapping and escape. There were the appropriate gasps and expressions of concern especially from those who had arrived after El.

Steve finished by saying, "I think we should all show the pastor how glad we are he's here safe and sound."

The congregation clapped and a few shouted "Amen." To El's surprise, Wayne McCarty stood up, still clapping. The rest of the congregation did likewise.

El stood. This time, tears welled in his eyes. He hoped he didn't cry. "Thank you all. I want you to know that it's only through God's providence that I'm here."

There was another round of applause. El smiled to the group and motioned them to sit down. The applause waned and people sat. El started to sit down but Steve stopped him.

"Won't you lead us in the opening prayer, Pastor?" Steve asked.

El nodded. "Dear Lord, thank you for bringing us

together tonight to share our hurts and our joys. We all sin and fall short, Lord, but you are always merciful. Thank you for that mercy. I want to thank you especially for taking care of me and bringing me safely through the valley of the shadow." El remembered that brush-filled ravine. "Thank you for all these dear people who have shared their love and concern for me. Be with them and guide them. Now, Lord, be with Steve as he brings the message tonight. Amen."

El sat down as Steve began the service. He jotted down the various prayer requests, so he could refer to them later. Some might require a follow up on his part. The service went smoothly. Steve brought a good lesson, and there was a lively discussion afterward. *Better than me,* El thought ruefully.

Steve closed the meeting with a prayer. El stood to leave. Wayne reached over and touched his arm.

"Stay a minute, Pastor."

El sat back down. Most of the people had left the hall. A few were still talking in twos and threes, but they were well out of earshot.

"What is it, Brother Wayne?"

"Several of the deacons have been talking to each other. We're real concerned about all the publicity that the church has been getting. You know it's not good."

"I know. It bothers me, too."

Wayne nodded vigorously. "I knew you would understand. I'm sorry to bring this up right now, but the sooner you know the better. I don't like going behind someone's back."

El tried to look receptive, even though, his stomach was already getting queasy. Maybe it was just the ham.

"Well," Wayne continued, "you see some of the deacons thought that maybe if you took a leave of absence for a month or two until all of this is cleared up . . . well, it might take some of the heat off the church."

"I see," El said. His stomach churned now, and he

felt a rising nausea. A leave of absence could easily become permanent. "What do you think, Brother Wayne?"

Wayne looked away. "Well, I think they're probably right about taking heat off the church. You know that state legislator, Depew, has been making speeches about us. About your preaching, how liberal it is, and how it's not Baptist. I'm sorry, but he has."

El's nausea disappeared. Fear gave way to anger. "You're going to let some outsider decide what you think of your pastor?"

"No, no, no. It's just that he calls attention to us, to the church. If you were gone for a while, he might find something else to fuss about."

El said nothing. When Wayne had first spoken, El had almost agreed, but he would not let that politician run him out of his own church.

"What if I don't take a leave of absence?"

"It's your choice, Pastor. I'll back you, if you stay. I am the deacon chairman."

That surprised El. He had not expected Wayne to support him at all. "Thanks, Wayne. I appreciate that. Give me some time to think about it. Okay?"

"Sure. One thing though." Wayne looked at the table. "What?"

"No pay. If you take the leave, we won't be able to pay you. We'll need an interim pastor, so we'll need your salary to pay him."

"I see," El said. "Steve could cover for a short time. You wouldn't need anyone right away."

Wayne continued to look at the table. "Sure, we haven't really talked out all the details." Wayne raised his head and looked at El. "Listen, if you decide to do it, I'll make sure you get at least a month's pay."

"What if I just resign?" El asked.

Wayne pursed his lips. "We're not asking for that. Don't do anything hasty."

"No, I won't. I'll give you my decision tomorrow."

"Good, there's that deacon's meeting tomorrow evening to discuss what's been going on. I was about to cancel it, but I won't now; that would just give things time to fester. You can come if you want to."

El had a hard time controlling his anger now. "How come I didn't know about this meeting?"

Wayne looked genuinely surprised. "You were supposed to. It was scheduled before you disappeared. Brother Bill said he would tell you. He didn't?"

El shook his head. "No, he didn't, but I'm not coming anyway. I'm not going to defend myself against something I haven't done. I will give you my decision before that meeting."

Wayne nodded and stood as did El. Abruptly, Wayne held out his hand. "Whatever happens, Pastor, I don't believe you are involved in murder or drug pushing."

"Thanks, Wayne." El shook his hand. For the first time since he came to Hill Country, El appreciated his deacon chairman.

El left Fellowship Hall. Just outside the door, a small knot of people had gathered. Otis Wheeler stepped out as El passed.

"Pastor, we want to talk to you," Otis said.

El's queasiness returned. Otis Wheeler, too.

"Pastor, we want you to know that not everyone feels the way Bill Gunter does. We'll stand behind you. Don't do anything foolish."

Otis's words brought tears to El's eyes, again. He hoped the light was poor enough that Otis could not see them. El reached out his hand to Otis.

"Thank you, Brother Otis, thank you."

Otis nodded and smiled. "It will be all right, Pastor."

El could say no more. He nodded to Otis and the others and walked on. There were good people in this church.

As he drove home, he tried to think clearly, but he

was not very successful. He was praying when he pulled into his drive. It didn't seem to help his inner pain. When he got out of his car, he heard something move. Were the drug dealers back?

"Who's there?"

No answer.

El's heart pounded as he made his way to the steps. He switched on the outside light. Something moved over by the storage room. It was too small to be a man.

El sighed in relief. Probably a varmint of some kind. He picked up a handful of pebbles to throw as he walked toward the storage room. A kitten, an orange and white kitten, peered around the corner. It had enormous ears.

How did it get here? El shook his head. Someone must have dumped it. The kitten mewed. It must be hungry.

"Kitty, kitty, kitty," El called.

The little cat looked at him uncertainly and mewed again. El repeated his call. This time, the kitten walked toward him very slowly. El squatted down, and the kitten stopped. El called again, but the kitten advanced no further. After some time, El's knee began to ache. He straightened up slowly hoping not to scare the kitten, but it retreated to the side of the storage room.

El shook his head. He couldn't leave a kitten down here. How could he catch it? Maybe, if he had some food with which to entice the little beast. He remembered some cold chicken in the refrigerator. El went in to the house. He shredded some of the chicken and put it in a saucer. He knew better than to offer milk to the kitten. At its age, it might not be able to handle it. Milk gave grown cats diarrhea, and El didn't know at what age kittens stopped being able to digest it.

El remembered all too well how he had learned that fact about cats. A large, white, male cat named Milton had lived with El for many years. Milton had turned the bathroom of El's first apartment into a giant latrine when

El, in his ignorance, had given him some milk.

El had been baffled and afraid Milton was sick. He had called his mother for advice. His mother was a cat lover from way back. The first question she asked was whether he had given Milton milk. When he said yes, she laughed. After she stopped laughing, she told him what the problem was. Cleaning up Milton's mess had been enough. El never made that mistake again. He wouldn't make it now.

Milton had died at the age of eighteen, just after El took the job with Hill Country. He had decided that he was too busy for a cat and had not gotten another. Maybe it was time.

El went back under the house with his saucer of chicken. At first, he didn't see the kitten, then he spotted it in the shadows. Those ears made it look more like a little fox than a cat. He crouched again and called, holding the saucer at arms length. The kitten once again approached, but stopped about three feet away. Moving slowly, El took a piece of chicken and tossed it to the cat. It shied away, but then came back. It sniffed the chicken before it gobbled it down. El held out the saucer again. This time the kitten came to it.

El let it eat a couple of bites then he reached down and grabbed it, fully expecting to be clawed or bitten. The kitten squalled and twisted, but did nothing else. El tightened his grip slightly and brought him to his chest.

"Come on, we'll go in." Carefully, El headed up the steps. He could feel the kitten's heart race, but it didn't struggle. When he reached his front door he knew he had a problem. He still had the saucer of chicken in one hand. The kitten was in the other. He could not open the door. Carefully, he put the chicken down. He didn't want the kitten to take off now. He opened the door one-handed. Once inside, he closed the door behind him and headed for the bathroom. He put the kitten in the shower. It retreated to the corner of the stall.

El closed the bathroom door and then retrieved the chicken from outside. He put it on the floor of the shower. The kitten moved to it and started to eat immediately. Now, for some water for the little cat. El got a cereal bowl and filled it with water. He put it beside the food bowl; the kitten did not stop eating.

The next thing was a litter box. El thought for a moment. *Where did I put Milton's?*

A few minutes later, he found it in the storage room along with a half-used bag of cat sand. He soon had the box installed in the bathroom. The kitten had finished eating and now was washing its face.

"Nice kitty. What are we going to call you?"

The cat stopped licking and stared at El. Then it stood up and slowly began to investigate its surroundings. El watched. Investigate, that was it.

"We'll call you Holmes." El said. "If you are a boy, that is." In the excitement, El hadn't checked. Holmes picked that moment to look behind the clothes hamper, which put his rump in front of El. "Holmes, it is."

El stood up. The cat had taken his mind off his own problems for a while. Now he had to face them. He left the kitten and went into the living room. He dropped onto the sofa.

"Dear Lord, what shall I do? What shall I do?"

▲15▼

EL WOKE EARLY. There was a strange sound. *What was it?* There it was again. A thud. El remembered, the kitten, but it was supposed to be shut in the bathroom. From the sounds, Holmes was loose in the house. El got up and stumbled toward the last thud. The kitten was exploring the living room. The thuds occurred when he hopped off one piece of furniture and headed for another. El watched him for a moment.

A four-shelf bookcase was his current target, but he was not having much luck. The little cat paced back and forth in front of it looking for a way to climb up. El chuckled, and Holmes immediately turned to look at him.

"Well, you seem to have made yourself at home. I thought I shut you in the bathroom last night." The bathroom door often opened unless it was locked, and El had not wanted to lock the door last night, so he had taken the chance. He made a quick tour of the house. There did not seem to be any damage. He hoped there had not been any sandbox misses.

"I'll get dressed and go get you some food, then we probably better pay a visit to the vet."

The kitten peered at him as he talked as if trying to decipher the strange words.

El dressed quickly, then drove to a nearby convenience store. Cat food there cost a fortune, but at least it was fast. He returned with two cans of a brand unknown to him, enough to last until he could get to a regular and cheaper grocery store.

Holmes had no doubts about the unknown brand. He ate the food El dished up with relish. Watching the kitten, El realized he was hungry. He fixed a quick breakfast.

He was finishing clearing the table when the phone rang. It was Martha. She started talking as soon as he said hello.

"Sorry to call so early, but you didn't say when you'd be in today. I've had a couple of calls by people wanting to talk to you. Mrs. Boyd and Mr. McCarty. Mr. McCarty said there was no hurry, but Mrs. Boyd is only here for the morning, then she is heading back to Dallas. She said she would be at her house from about ten until noon."

El was finally able to speak. "That's okay, Martha. I'll run an errand, then I'll go see Mrs. Boyd. Would you call her and tell her I'll be at her house about ten-thirty?"

"Of course. Will you be in after that?"

"Yes, I should be at the office for the rest of the day."

"Good, good-bye."

"Good-bye," El said. He had decided not to let people know that his errand was a visit to a veterinarian, not when his job was in jeopardy. He felt queasy again. He wished he could forget about his conversation with Wayne McCarty. He could not, but he was going to take care of his new cat. A small act of defiance.

He went back to the storage room and found Milton's old carrying case. It was a wire and wood one, not one of the newfangled plastic ones. El took it upstairs and used a paper towel to wipe out the cobwebs and dust. He checked the corners again when he'd finished. Brown recluse spiders regularly tried to set up housekeeping in his cabin. He didn't want one hiding in the corner of the carrier to bite Holmes later. A bite from a brown recluse caused the tissue around the wound to die. There wasn't enough of Holmes to survive that.

Satisfied that the carrier was pest-free, he lined the bottom with paper towels, then went in search of the kitten. He found Holmes exploring his bedroom. El scooped him up and took him back to the carrier. Holmes purred all the way. Quickly, El deposited him in the carrier. The little kitten looked confused as El closed the carrier door. He huddled down and turned big eyes on El.

In a few minutes, they were on their way. Holmes crouched in the case on the seat next to El, his eyes still wide.

"It's okay," El said.

Holmes obviously did not believe him.

El decided not to use a local vet, even though it would be quicker. Instead, he headed for his old veterinarian in north Austin. Twenty minutes later, El sat in the waiting room. He was lucky, no one was ahead of him.

As he relaxed, Wayne McCarty's conversation ran through his mind. El had made his decision; he hoped it was the right one. He would not take a leave of absence. If he were arrested, he would resign. If he were not arrested, then he'd give Bill Gunter and his pals a battle. He had seen more than one senior minister win such a fight. He could, too. If he were arrested, he would assume that was God's way of showing him he did not belong in the ministry.

"Mr. Littlejohn, you may come in now."

El followed the receptionist into a small examining room. There was a small sink against one wall, cabinets, some paraphernalia, medicines, and towels on the countertop. In the middle of the room was a blue formica-topped table. One matching blue, plastic-covered chair occupied a corner. A second door led to the rear of the clinic.

"Dr. Mabry will be in in a moment."

El nodded. He put the carrier on the table and opened its door. Holmes did not come out. El reached in and pulled him out. The kitten crouched on the table.

"Hello, what have we here," Dr. Mabry said as he entered. "Finally got yourself another cat."

Dr. Mabry had nursed Milton through his last illness and had cared for the Littlejohns's pets for the past ten years. Before that, Dr. Mabry's father and his partner had looked after the numerous family and childhood pets. El had known this Dr. Mabry, Jim, since he took over the practice. He trusted him.

"Turned up at my house. I guess I'll keep him. He needs a checkup and his shots, if he's okay," El said.

Jim nodded and began his exam. El was surprised how behaved Holmes was. He trembled, but didn't bite or scratch.

Finished, Dr. Mabry stroked the cat. "He looks to be in pretty good condition." He smiled. "He's good-natured, too. He's purring right now. We need to draw some blood to test for feline leukemia, okay?"

"Of course," said El.

"I'll be back in a minute." Jim scooped up Holmes and left the examining room.

El sat down in the room's one chair. What would happen to Holmes if he were arrested? Nothing. His mother would only be too glad to add to her menagerie of cats, dogs, and birds.

If he were arrested . . . He was innocent. Why should he be arrested? Because it would be very easy for the sheriff to pin the murder on him. He'd have to do what he'd started to do before he was kidnapped, find out who in his church had been making the drugs. If that man had not killed Leroy, then perhaps he could tell El the most likely candidate.

El started through the congregation in his mind. Maybe he could figure it out himself without Thornhill's notes. He was still working on his mental checklist when Dr. Mabry returned.

"He's a good cat. We got the blood with no trouble. I can give him all his shots, but leukemia, if you want. Or you can wait for the lab results."

"Give him those shots."

"Fine."

Holmes took the shots with an air of stoic resignation, but he scuttled into the carrier when Dr. Mabry released him.

"Thanks a lot. Shall I call tomorrow for the results?"

"Yes, after ten."

El nodded and went out to the receptionist. She had a white plastic bag labeled "Preventive Health Care for Your Cat" in blue on the counter.

"For Holmes," she said. "That'll be thirty-five dollars all together."

El nodded and wrote a check. A few minutes later, he was on his way back home. Once there, he released Holmes and opened the second can of food. Holmes ate as if it were the first meal of the day. El petted him, the tiny rump rose slightly. El smiled, then sobered. He better get going. He said he would be at Mrs. Boyd's house at ten-thirty.

There was only one car in the drive when he reached the Boyds's. He assumed it was Melanie's. He rang the bell. Melanie answered the door. She looked much more her old self, neat and fresh-scrubbed.

"Oh, I'm so glad you came, Pastor. I wanted to talk to you."

"That's what Martha said. May I come in?"

For a moment, Melanie seemed confused, then she nodded. "Of course. My mother's here. We left the kids with friends in Dallas."

El followed Melanie into the living room. It looked

very different than a few days before. All the small things that spoke of living were gone. Only the furniture and several cardboard boxes remained.

"The movers are coming this afternoon. I'm not taking everything, just what I want, and I'm putting the house on the market."

"Then you're leaving here permanently."

"Yes, I think it's better for the kids. And me, too."

"I'm sorry," El said as he sat down on the sofa.

Melanie sat down beside him. "The newspapers and the TV have been real bad. And that awful state legislator. The day of the funeral he went on TV and said that Leroy's soul would burn in hell. The Dallas newspaper quoted him the next day, too."

"I'm sorry, I didn't know Depew did that. No man can know whether someone else has gone to heaven or to hell. Like I told you before, if Leroy was saved, then no matter what he did, he has gone to heaven." El wondered how Depew could think he had the right to judge someone he had never met.

Melanie nodded. "When I think about it, I know you're right. But when I hear that man . . . He's so convincing."

"I know. Was that what you wanted to talk about?"

Melanie shook her head. "Lieutenant Coronado questioned me again just before I left for Dallas. I thought you better know what he was asking."

"Oh," El said, trying to sound calm while his heart thudded so hard that Melanie must surely have heard it.

"He wanted to know if you and I were having an affair. If Leroy had found out."

El sat back. That idea had never entered his head, but he could see how it had Coronado's.

"I told him that was absurd. That you and I had only talked a few times before Leroy was killed. That I hardly knew you."

"That's the truth."

"I know, but I still thought you should know. Pastor, don't let Leroy reach you from the grave."

"Don't worry, Sister Melanie. I'm sure Lieutenant Coronado will soon find the real murderer."

"Yes, but what if a rumor about us got started. It could ruin your career."

El blinked. He honestly had not thought of that. He was so worried about being arrested for Leroy's murder that he had thought of no other consequences.

"It's not true. That's all that matters. Now, you don't worry about me. I'm going to be fine."

"That's what I've been telling her, Preacher." Mrs. Woods stood in the hall doorway.

"It's good advice," El smiled. "You listen to your mother, Melanie."

Melanie nodded, but her eyes still held uncertainty. El realized she was a very attractive woman, a very vulnerable woman at this moment. No wonder Coronado had thought there might be an affair in progress.

El stood. "I'll be going, but if there is anything I can do or the church can, don't hesitate to call."

"We won't," said Mrs. Woods. Melanie only nodded. She did not get up.

El left.

On his way to the church, El wondered if any of the congregation thought there was something between Melanie Boyd and himself. Under different circumstances, he could have asked Steve, but right now he didn't want to plant any thoughts in Steve's head that were not already there. There was no one else he could think of to ask.

"Lord, I'm really in trouble. What should I do? I don't want to leave my church, but I don't want to hurt it either."

El crossed the Pedernales River. He was sure he hadn't crossed it the night he was kidnapped. That meant the house where he'd been held was between Austin and the Pedernales. On the lake or close to it because he'd seen boat lights, at least he thought he remembered boat lights. The memory of that night was pretty dim. If he could just remember the sequence of sounds the roads made just before they reached the house. They had stayed on the highway or a well-paved road a long time. Maybe if he drove around a while, he might remember or hear the same sounds, better yet maybe he'd see the house. He was sure he could recognize the house.

The road to the county park was just ahead, El turned. It wouldn't hurt to try. There were several smaller roads leading off of it. Had they been on one of those?

The road dead-ended at the park. Dust swirled on the other side of the entrance. This time of year everything dried up from the lack of rain. El turned around. He did not think his kidnappers had taken him there. He headed back toward Highway 71. He turned down the first side road he came to. It led into a small subdivision. El circled through it. Lake Travis would not be visible from any of these homes, and they were too small anyway. Their brown lawns said that most here were too poor to water.

El returned to Highway 71. He took the next two turn-offs with no better luck. One led to a small group of houses with green lawns and trimmed bushes. It seemed out of place with the scraggly cedar and dry grass just a turn away. The second led him on a twisting tour of the remoter parts west of Lake Travis. He finally decided that this search was silly. He'd never retrace that ride of Monday night. He better see what was going on at church, see what he could do to keep his job.

▲16▼

I T WAS A little after twelve when El turned into the church parking lot. It was empty. Martha and Steve must have left for lunch. *Where was Harry?* There was no sign of his old pickup. Harry usually brought his lunch and ate here. El parked in front of the office. He was not surprised that the office door was locked. He unlocked it and walked in.

El stood for a moment in the doorway. How seldom he really looked at the place. The walls and ceiling were an off-white. The floor was a vinyl tile in a marble pattern. Martha kept it neat. Harry kept it clean. There were two gray filing cabinets on the west wall, next to the entrance to Steve's office. Martha's metal desk sat in the middle of the room. On one side was her calendar, on the other her phone. Her typewriter was on a table to the left. Everything had its place. Everything but him.

El shook his head. What was wrong with him? He had a place, his office was directly behind Martha's desk, and it was time he got to work. Maybe that would take his mind off his problems. He went in his office, leaving his door ajar so he could hear anyone coming in the front door, and sat down at his desk. He looked through his IN box quickly. There was nothing urgent. He dropped it all back in its box.

For a moment, he sat. He thought about calling some

of the church members he knew would be on his side. No, he had done enough for now. He'd wait till he heard from Wayne McCarty. Until then, he would look at those membership files again. He was in the middle of the Ms when he heard the outside door open.

"El, are you here?" Steve called. Steve must have seen his office door was open.

"Yes, I'm in my office. Come in."

Steve appeared in the doorway. "Hi there. Did you get by to see Mrs. Boyd?"

"Yes, she and her mother." El was careful to add Mrs. Wood, no use creating gossip. "Sister Melanie just wanted to thank me and the church for everything. She's leaving permanently. Thinks it's better for the kids."

"Probably is," Steve said with a sigh. "Too bad." He walked in without asking and sat down in the chair against the far wall. "That take all morning?" he asked as he leaned back, rocking the chair onto its rear legs.

El looked at him and resisted the urge to tell him not to sit in that chair like that. It always annoyed him when someone sat in a chair like that. El always expected them to tip over. El focused on Steve's question. It seemed innocent enough. Why not tell him the truth or at least part of it? He'd leave out his fruitless search for the kidnapper's house.

"No, I found a kitten at my house last night. Took it into the vet this morning to get it checked and get shots. It's a pretty little cat, orange and white."

"Don't let Linda hear about it. She's always adopting strays."

"Not this one. I'm going to keep him. He'll be company. I named him Holmes."

Steve shook his head. "You don't need a cat for company. You need a wife. It would be much easier on you if you'd get married."

It was El's turn to shake his head. "I haven't had a date in a year. Who'd I marry?"

Steve gazed at the ceiling. "Well, for starters, there are several very attractive, young women in our congregation that have the hots for you."

"Steve, you shouldn't say that."

"Come on, El. You must have noticed the young women that have joined since you became pastor. Each hopes that she will be the one that catches you. We've added more single women than new families." Steve laughed.

"I don't think that's true." El wasn't about to admit that he hadn't paid attention to the numbers. However, he had noticed a couple of those gals. As pastor, he had figured he better not get involved with a member of the congregation. "Besides, Steve, no one is catching me. I'll choose my own wife."

Steve frowned, brought the front legs of his chair to the floor, and looked El in the eye. "Seriously, El, you know that some of the members are uneasy with a single man as pastor. People think strange things."

"Such as . . ." El was not going to give Steve any help, but he knew what Steve was talking about. His boss at his previous job had often told El that being single hurt his career. A church liked to call a couple, sort of getting two for the price of one. A pastor's wife was supposed to work for the church, but not for pay. El wondered how ministers' wives felt about that. He brought his attention back to Steve.

Steve shifted his gaze to the floor. "Well, that an unmarried man has something wrong with him. I mean, a minister has to be celibate unless he's married."

"But he can date."

"That's different."

El studied his assistant. Steve was not telling him the real problem. El thought he could guess, but perversely, he wanted to make Steve tell.

"What would be wrong with such a man?"

Steve chewed his lower lip and did not look up.

"Well, just what I said, but also, you know, some people think that you might be gay."

Steve looked as if he had eaten a lemon when he said gay. El couldn't help but laugh. Just what he thought. What a joke. Coronado believed he was having an affair with a deacon's wife while some of his congregation thought he was a homosexual. You had to see the humor in life sometimes or break down and cry.

"It's not funny. Gossip like that could cost you your job."

El stopped laughing. Steve looked so hurt. "Sorry, Steve, I know, but I can assure you I'm not gay. Far from it. I just haven't met a woman I want to spend the rest of my life with. Do many of the congregation think I'm gay?"

Steve shook his head. "No, only two or three, as far as I know. The others don't take it seriously."

So, thought El, this topic has been discussed at some length. The things they didn't teach you at seminary. Let's see, some of his congregation thought he was a murderer, some thought he was a drug dealer, and two or three thought he was gay. He had no doubt which was considered the worst.

"That's good. I'd appreciate it, if you'd set the record straight with those two or three. I can give you the names of a couple of old girlfriends from the time before I felt God's call. They could prove my sexual orientation."

Steve wiggled in his chair.

Seeing Steve's discomfort, El couldn't resist going on. "Although if I were a celibate homosexual, why should anyone care?"

Steve actually paled. "Don't joke about such an abomination."

El contemplated his friend. Did they live in the same era? El knew that at least two men in the congregation were gay. In the course of the last year, he had had to counsel each about the loss of either a lover or friend to AIDS. Obviously, Steve did not know about their sexual orientation. *Oh, Lord, what if they had gone to Steve instead of him?*

El sighed. "I'm not sure we should be so quick to condemn. From what I've been reading, a homosexual can't help being that way."

"The Bible doesn't say that."

El gave up. He didn't want to fight with Steve, not today. "You're right. Now, do you want the names of my old girlfriends?"

Steve sat forward, licked his lips, and once again, looked El in the eye. "I couldn't talk to one of your girlfriends. Ask them about . . . No way. I mean, wouldn't they be ashamed?"

"Steve, these women were in college with me in the early seventies. Things were pretty free and easy. They're not Baptists."

"Oh, I see," Steve said.

El suppressed the urge to say a bad word. He had added that last statement just to see how Steve would react. He actually did not know what faith, if any, those girls had practiced. He had known a couple of Baptist coeds casually. Both had dated friends of his. From their comments, those girls were no different from the ones he dated. But he'd let Steve keep his illusions. Sometimes, it scared him that a minister like Steve could harbor such ideas. Another thought came unbidden. *Maybe Steve thinks correctly. Maybe you're the one that's wrong.*

"Enough of this. I've got to work on Sunday's sermon. Anything else?"

"No, just wanted to chat. Talk to you later." Steve stood up and smiled a rather strained smile.

El had a sudden urge to ask Steve if he had been a virgin when he married, but he did not. Under his breath, El said, "Sorry, Lord. I shouldn't bait him. He's sincere,

I know. He wants what is best for this church. It's just that he and I are so different.''

As Steve left El's office, Martha stuck her head in the door. ''I'm back. I'll get the phones.''

''That's fine. There weren't any calls while I was here.''

Martha smiled and left, closing the door behind her. El stared at it for a moment. He looked at the file on his desk. He really did need to start on his sermon. He shoved the file away and got out a yellow pad. He began to jot down possible topics and Bible verses.

He was still doing that when Wayne McCarty called. Wayne got directly to the point. ''Well, Pastor, what have you decided?''

''I'm going to stay, and I won't take any leave of absence, Wayne. I've done absolutely nothing wrong. If the deacons think otherwise, then so be it.''

''Good enough for me, Pastor. I'll be in touch.''

''Okay. Good-bye, Brother Wayne.''

''Good-bye, Pastor.''

El sat for a moment. He just didn't want to work on the sermon anymore. He dropped the pad on the table. He'd make another try at finding his kidnappers. He gathered up the membership files. He'd take them with him. Maybe later, he could find something in them.

On his way out, he told Martha that he'd be in in the morning. He had some business to attend to now.

Once in his car, El drove home. When he got there, he dropped the files on the sofa and petted Holmes, then returned to his Mustang. He didn't want to waste time at home. He drove back to the highway. *Which way had the kidnappers turned?* Not toward town, he was almost sure. El turned left, that had to be the way they went. He tried to recall how long it had been before they had turned off the highway, he couldn't, so he turned at the first road toward Lake Travis and followed it. It petered out quickly. El retraced his route and tried the next road.

He had found some interesting places by the time he decided to call it quits, but nothing that jogged his memory. Finding that house was probably impossible. He'd do better to try to find the member of the congregation that had helped Leroy. He'd finish those files tonight, but he was beginning to think they would not give him the information he needed. If he couldn't find it in the files, he'd have to do it on his own. He must find Leroy's accomplice.

El started toward home, then remembered the kitten. He might as well get a supply of cat food. He stopped at the local supermarket and picked up some kitten food and toys and some frozen dinners for himself.

Holmes was asleep in El's chair when he got home. The kitten woke up, stretched, then looked expectantly at El. He seemed to have made himself at home. El opened a can of the kitten food and gave Holmes fresh water. From the way Holmes attacked his food, you'd think he hadn't been fed all day. El got out another bowl and filled it with dry food. Now, Holmes could eat as much as he wanted when he wanted. El set that beside the canned food. Holmes did not even pause in his eating.

El put a frozen dinner in the microwave and turned on the TV. The six o'clock news was just starting. The third story of the evening began with a picture of Marcus Matthew Depew. He had been appointed to the Home Mission Board of the Southern Baptist Convention. El sat up. How could that man get such a post? The shot changed, Depew had called a press conference at the Capitol. A reporter asked Depew what this appointment meant to him.

"My appointment is just one of many marking a new era in the Southern Baptist denomination. We will restore the Bible to its rightful place in Southern Baptist churches. Soon we will rid ourselves of those liberal elements that do not believe in the Great Book."

El wanted to throw something at the TV. Instead he satisfied himself by going to the bathroom. When he returned, the weather was on. After the news, El sat down to eat his supper.

"Dear Lord, thank you for this food. Use it for the nourishment of my body. Lord, forgive me for my ill feelings toward him. Help me to practice brotherly love, even though I don't want to. Amen."

▲17▼

EL PULLED OUT the last file he had brought home from the office. He worked through it methodically. Finished, he closed it. There were just no indications who Leroy's partner had been. He had hoped that Reverend Thornhill had noted some character defect or suspected someone of criminal activity, but there was nothing in the files. After reading all of Thornhill's notes, El was not sure the man would have written anything that blunt.

One thing for sure, from the notes he left, the old man had been an astute judge of character. Too bad he wasn't here now. El would have liked to talk to him about the church. *Had Thornhill had trouble with Gunter?* His notes didn't tell.

What could El do now? Figure out who killed Leroy himself? He went over all the events and clues that he knew. Leroy had been counting the morning offering when he had been surprised by someone, but no money had been taken. El closed his eyes. Maybe, Leroy had not been counting money. Maybe, he had been back in the linen closet getting out the dope, then whoever had killed him had taken it.

El opened his eyes. There was no proof that there had been any drugs in that closet at the time Leroy was shot, but the intruder that attacked El that evening had been after something. What? It made sense if a batch of drugs had been delivered Sunday morning. El's kidnappers had claimed to be looking for a missing batch of drugs. With Leroy dead, the supplier would want to get rid of the drugs or pass them on to the dealer himself. If El was right, his attacker was also Leroy's supplier.

Who was Leroy's supplier? Who? Who was always in that area besides Leroy?

Calvin Roller. El shook his head. Not Calvin; Calvin was too obvious. Just because he was chairman of the Baptism Committee and in charge of baptismal supplies did not mean he was in cahoots with Leroy. Besides, Lieutenant Coronado hadn't been concerned about Calvin. If Calvin were the drug chemist, Coronado would have picked up on it.

But now, El remembered seeing Calvin near the closet frequently. More often than needed? El didn't know. He'd just never paid attention to Calvin. Calvin was one of those people who seemed more a fixture in the church than a member of the church.

From all appearances, Calvin barely knew Leroy. El had never seen them sit together on Wednesday nights, Sundays, or at deacons' meetings. Calvin didn't appear to have a lot of money either. El reached for the files again.

He flipped to the Rs and found Calvin's name. He had read his page once. There were a few of Thornhill's handwritten notes. "Hard worker, but low self-esteem. Feels trapped in his job. Always glad to help out in church."

That didn't help. He looked at the typewritten entries. Calvin worked for the state, the Parks and Wildlife agency and had a B.A. in Biology from Texas A & M. Biology. Calvin was bound to have taken some chemistry courses. Why had he missed that the first time through these files? Because he could not conceive of Calvin as running a clandestine lab. Calvin was a man to depend upon, a kind, caring man. He could never manufacture illegal drugs.

El had been to Calvin's modest home, had supper with him and his wife. Calvin had no children. There had been no evidence of extra money, of a man living beyond his means.

El shut the file. This was ridiculous. Here he was suspecting one of his best church members. Better think about something else.

El turned his attention to Holmes who was busily stalking one of his new kitten toys, a plastic ball with a bell in it. The little cat pounced on the ball and sent it rolling. It jingled merrily. Holmes then went tearing after it and batted it in the opposite direction. El watched the kitten play and slowly relaxed.

After several minutes of watching Holmes, El returned to the problem. Maybe Calvin would have an idea about who could use the baptismal robes for passing drugs. Calvin might even have seen something suspicious. Coronado would have questioned him already, but Calvin might be more relaxed with El. Besides, he needed to get to know Calvin better, not think of him as a fixture.

El reopened the file and found Calvin's home phone. His watch said a little after nine; not too late. El dialed Calvin's number.

Calvin's wife, Edna, answered. "This is Brother El, how are you this evening?"

"I'm just fine, Pastor. And you?"

"Just fine, could I speak to Calvin?"

"He's not here, Pastor. He went to the deacons' meeting. Can I help you?"

"No, Sister Edna, I wanted to ask Calvin something about his work on the Baptism Committee. I forgot about the deacons' meeting. Could you take a message?"

"Sure, Pastor."

"Tell him I wanted to talk to him about the robe with pockets. He can call me if he gets in before eleven."

"The robe with pockets. I didn't know those robes came with pockets."

"They don't usually."

"Oh." Edna Roller sounded confused. "I'll give him the message."

"Thanks. Good-bye."

"Good-bye."

El turned on the TV. He idly switched channels. Nothing appeared worth watching. Holmes was still chasing his ball but not in the living room. El could hear its jingle from the bedroom. That might be a problem when he went to bed, but maybe Holmes would get tired before then. El finally let the TV stay on the local PBS station. There was a British mystery on. El watched it. When it ended at ten, he switched to the local news.

He watched to see if there was any mention of Hill Country. He was relieved when there was none. The weather report was just coming on when the phone rang. El picked it up.

"This is Calvin Roller, Pastor. My wife said you'd called."

"That's right, I . . ."

Before El could say more, Calvin interrupted. "She gave me your message. Listen she doesn't know anything about it. Can we meet somewhere to talk?"

"Sure. Where would you like to meet?"

"How about the pizza place on 71 near the church?"

"That'll be fine."

"Good, I'll meet you there in fifteen minutes." Calvin hung up.

El stared at the phone. Why did Calvin feel it was so urgent to meet?

Suddenly, El felt ill. His first guess must have been correct. Calvin was mixed up in the drug ring. He must think that El was on to him. *Dear Lord, a man like Calvin making drugs.*

Another thought drove the sickness away. It was replaced with fear. Could Calvin be setting him up? El realized he had to take the chance. He had to know what had been going on in his church, and he had to stop it.

Ten minutes later, El pulled into a vacant parking space at the pizza place. He did not see Calvin's car, a dark blue Chevy, anywhere. He'd wait in his car a while before going in.

El waited only a couple of minutes before Calvin pulled in a few cars down. El got out and walked over to Calvin's auto. Calvin got out slowly. El could tell from his demeanor that he'd been right about the drug making. Why hadn't he noticed earlier? Calvin's eyes seemed dull, haunted, and his shoulders were stooped even more than usual. The man carried a heavy load.

El did not hold out his hand. Instead he said, "Good evening, Brother Calvin."

Calvin's eyes darted from side to side. Checking for the law?

"Good evening, Pastor," Calvin said. "Let's go inside."

El nodded. He preferred to be with a crowd, too.

A few minutes later, they sat across from each other in a booth toward the back of the dining room. The booths on either side were empty. They'd gotten a couple of soft drinks before they sat down. Now, Calvin stared at his. He wouldn't meet El's gaze.

"In God's name, Calvin, how did you get mixed up in a mess like this?" El asked.

"Leroy asked me." Calvin looked only at the tabletop.

"Why did you go along?"

Calvin raised his head and met El's eyes for the first time. "Leroy was going to get someone to make those drugs, and if I didn't, then someone else would."

El shook his head, appalled at the rationalization. "That's no reason. You could've turned Leroy in to the sheriff. Drugs destroy people, they're evil."

Tears filmed Calvin's blue eyes. "I know that, but I figured I could make a really pure drug. I'd read where addicts died or got brain damage from the impurities in the drugs because no one had any quality control. So, I was real careful; my stuff was 99 percent pure. Leroy got it tested at one of those California labs."

El heard the pride in Calvin's voice, pride at making a pure evil. *Dear Lord, if a man like Calvin can get caught up in the drug trade, what about the rest of us?*

"How long have you been doing this?" El asked.

"For about three years."

El felt a little ashamed at the relief those words brought. At least the drug dealing had started before he knew either man. But Calvin never flashed any money. His lifestyle gave no hint of his drug revenues.

"What did you do with the money?" El studied the man across from him.

"I put some in a savings account. The rest I hid behind the paneling in my den. I didn't spend any of it. I'm just two years from retirement. I planned to take the money and leave the country. No one would know where I got it then."

"God would." Whatever else El might not know about Calvin, he did know that Calvin was devout man, a God-fearing man.

Calvin's mouth twisted. His eyes again darted from side to side. "I asked for forgiveness. You said He forgives all sins, if we ask."

"But that doesn't mean he gives permission. If you keep on doing it, you're not asking for forgiveness."

Calvin again closed his eyes. He looked on the verge of tears.

"Does your wife know?" El asked.

Calvin shook his head. "Of course not; she'd never

allow it. I was going to tell her that a distant relative died and left me the money."

El sighed. What should he tell Calvin? "Calvin, you have to turn yourself in to the sheriff."

"I can't. I can't go to jail." Calvin opened his eyes and blinked at El. There were tears in them. "I'll give all the money to the church."

El shook his head. "No, Calvin, you can't bribe God. Jesus never said he'd let us escape the consequences of our acts, only that he would be with us through whatever came. Calvin, I'll go with you to the sheriff, if you want me to."

"No, I'll go alone, if I go."

"You can't keep doing this. Calvin, I don't think I've ever said this to anyone, but what you are doing is truly evil. I think you could endanger your soul. Quit, go to the sheriff."

Calvin nodded slowly. "Maybe you're right. With Leroy dead, I'd have to do business with the dealers directly. I don't want to do that."

El swallowed. Maybe Calvin could tell him who his kidnappers were. "Do you know who these dealers are?"

Calvin shook his head. "No, Leroy kept it to himself."

"Are they church members?"

Calvin frowned. "I don't think so. But the head guy is a Baptist. Leroy said something strange one time. That one of these days someone would cut his hair just like Samson. I think the guy is real powerful, maybe in his church. I dunno."

"Nothing else?"

"No, I'm sorry, Pastor."

El took a deep breath. There was one thing he needed to know. "Did you kill Leroy?"

Calvin's eyes widened. "Good God, no! I'm no murderer. I don't know who killed Leroy. I thought maybe you had.''

El let that last statement pass. "Did you make a delivery to Leroy that Sunday?''

"Yes, I put it in the baptismal robe. That was Leroy's idea because he counted the offering in the back every Sunday. He said no one would ever suspect. I didn't like using the church, but Leroy wouldn't do it any other way. He said we had to keep our distance, so no one would know.''

Calvin looked at El. "He didn't want his boss to know who made his drugs. Said it gave him a little leverage.''

"Anything unusual happen that last Sunday morning?'' El asked.

"No. Before church I went back and stuck the robe with the drugs at the bottom of the stack. Whoever killed Leroy must have taken the drugs. I checked Monday night and . . .'' Calvin's voice trailed away. He dropped his head.

"You're the one who attacked me.'' El had figured that out already. He knew he should be angry with Calvin, but all he felt was pity.

"I didn't mean to hurt you. I was just trying to get away.'' Calvin continued to gaze at the table. His finger drew an invisible circle. "The stuff was gone, like I said. The robe was still there, but the packets were gone.'' He looked at El as if he were the thief.

"How much dope was there?'' *Had Calvin met him just to find out if he had that last batch of drugs*? El hoped his suspicions didn't show.

Calvin shrugged. "Depending on how you cut it, probably close to a quarter of a million dollars' worth.''

El leaned back. *Two hundred fifty thousand dollars' worth of illicit drugs in the pockets of a baptismal robe. So much money, so much evil.*

"What did Leroy pay you for a batch?'' El asked.

"Twenty-five thousand dollars. I could have gotten

more if I'd dealt directly with the big guy, but I didn't want to deal with a criminal. Leroy took care of that."

El almost giggled. *Calvin didn't want to deal with a criminal. Dear Lord.*

"Calvin, you must turn yourself in. Tell all you know, if not . . ."

Calvin's eyes sparked. Spots of color appeared on his pale cheeks. "You going to turn me in? You're a minister. What I tell you is privileged."

El nodded. "I won't turn you in, at least not now, but what you did was wrong. It hurts so many people. Do you understand?"

"Yes, I'll quit. I won't make another batch ever. Just don't tell, Pastor. Think about my wife. I'll give the money to charity like I said."

El sighed. "I won't do anything until day after tomorrow. It's your soul, Calvin. I believe our acts can separate us from God, but our acts can bring us closer to Him too. You pray about it and so will I; if you haven't turned yourself in by then, we'll talk again."

"I'll pray, I will, Pastor. Thanks."

Calvin got up quickly and sidled away. El watched him. Was Calvin playing him for a fool? Perhaps he should go to the sheriff now. No. For Calvin's sake it would be better if he confessed on his own. El sighed, again. What would he do if Calvin didn't go to the sheriff?

On the way home, El went over his talk with Calvin. He hoped he had reached him.

"Dear Lord, I may not have said the right things, but you have it in your power to set Calvin straight. Help him to do the right thing. In Jesus's name, Amen."

▲18▼

HOLMES'S LIGHT FOOTSTEPS on his chest woke El. The clock said eight. El squinted at it. He had set the alarm for seven. He must have turned the alarm off, but he didn't remember doing it.

El was not surprised he overslept. Last night, he had replayed his conversation with Calvin over and over. Had he said the right things to Calvin? Should he have insisted then that they go the the sheriff? He just didn't know the answers. The last time he remembered looking at the clock it had been a little after two. He looked at the clock again. Last night's worries returned. What should he do about Calvin?

Holmes was busily prowling El's bed. El wiggled his toes under the sheet. The little cat's eyes grew big. He crouched, and his small body tensed. El wiggled his toes again. Holmes pounced and bit hard, inserting a row of needlelike teeth into El's big toe. El yipped and jerked his foot away. Frightened, Holmes bolted out of the room.

El climbed out of bed and stumbled after Holmes. "Here, kitty, kitty, kitty. I'm sorry. Come on, Holmes."

He paused at his bedroom door to check his toe. Blood spotted it in a couple of places. El walked gingerly into the living room favoring the toe.

There was no sign of an orange and white kitten. El

went to the pantry and took out a can of food. He popped the top. Before he could even get a saucer out, Holmes meowed at him from the floor. All was forgiven. *If only people could do it that easily,* El thought.

There was another more impatient meow.

"Okay, okay, I'm hurrying."

El got the saucer out, upended the food onto it, then placed it in front of the little cat. Holmes attacked it hungrily.

The saucer was empty by the time El dressed and was ready to leave. He'd skip breakfast this morning; he was too worried to eat. He gave Holmes fresh water and a pat before he left.

El got to the office by a quarter of nine. Martha greeted him with a smile, but the tiny furrows on her forehead told El she was worried.

"What's the matter?" El asked.

"Mr. McCarty's called twice. He wants you to call as soon as you get in."

"Is that the problem?" El didn't think that Martha would look so upset about his missing a couple of calls.

"No, Steve told me the deacons met last night. He said . . ." Martha looked down. There were tears in her eyes.

"That bad, huh?"

She nodded.

El patted her on the back. "Don't worry, everything will be fine. It's not as bad as it seems. I haven't left yet."

Martha sniffled. "Don't let them run you off. Stand your ground."

"I'm going to, Martha. I'm going to."

El went in to his office and sat down. He wondered how Steve had found out so quickly. After this was all over, he'd have to have a talk with Steve, if he were still the pastor.

Maybe he should leave the ministry. He could find a

job as a chemist. Maybe he could go back to school, get that doctorate. No, he didn't want it now. He wanted to be pastor of this church. He'd better call Wayne.

As El reached for the phone, it rang. He picked it up. "Hello, Pastor Littlejohn here."

"Good morning, Pastor. This is Wayne McCarty."

"Yes, Brother Wayne, I was about to call you."

"I'd like to come by your office, Pastor. When would be a good time?"

"Brother Wayne, you can tell me over the phone."

There was a long silence. "I prefer face to face, but maybe you're right. No use pussyfootin' around. Like I told you before, some of the deacons are concerned that you may not be the best man for Hill Country, that you don't project the right image. I mean, all this publicity, nothing like this happened before you were pastor."

"I see, Brother Wayne. Am I fired?"

"No, no, it hasn't gone that far yet. Last night was sort of a no confidence vote. They're leaving it up to you for now, but I think there's a majority leaning toward asking you to resign."

So, thought El, not a leave of absence, but resignation. "If I don't resign?"

"Nothing will happen for a while. I told them we had to give you some time. There's a pretty strong minority that want you to stay. They were pretty outspoken, so you've got at least six weeks to think it over. Look around for other prospects if you want to. After that . . . Well, it'll probably depend on how this mess turns out."

"As it stands right now, Wayne, I won't resign and I'll put up a fight to stay. I have done nothing wrong."

"That's your decision, Pastor, but don't be too hasty. Take the six weeks. It'll give things a chance to cool off."

El understood. Wayne was a better politician than he. If the murder was resolved, and El not implicated, the deacons would probably drop the matter. If he were arrested . . .

"I understand, Wayne. Six weeks. Thank you."

"Good, I'll tell them. Pastor, I . . ." Wayne hesitated.

"What Wayne?"

"I've got an invitation to a party at Senator Depew's place. Why don't you come along with me?"

El almost laughed. *Depew!* "I don't think so, Brother Wayne. I gather he doesn't like my sermons."

"I know what he's been saying, Pastor, but he's never met you. You might be able to change his mind."

"I doubt it. He has said some pretty bad things about me and the church."

"Okay, Pastor, I'll level with you. I don't think you have a chance of getting on the good side of Depew. Matter of fact, I had to wrangle the invitation just for myself. But there are going to be lots of prominent people there, especially Baptists. You go, and I'll spread the word that you went. Some of the deacons will be mighty impressed. If it comes to a showdown later that might make all the difference."

"When is this party?" El asked reluctantly.

"Tonight. Now, wait. Don't say no because it's short notice. I just found out about it yesterday myself. You don't have to stay. We can take our own cars, and you can leave anytime."

Wayne was right about the deacons, but El wasn't even sure he wanted to meet Depew or be in the same room with the man. If it would help him keep his job . . .

"Okay," El said. "What time?"

"The party starts at eight. Depew lives out past you, so I'll pick you up at eight. We don't want to be the first to arrive."

"Is it formal?"

"No, casual. Shirt and slacks or jeans."

"Good," El said. If the party was formal, El would

have backed out. "See you at eight, Wayne, good-bye."

"Good-bye, Pastor."

El put the phone down slowly. Relief like the first sip of a good wine flowed through his body. He had just received a vote of no confidence, but he hadn't been fired. Many things could change in six weeks. Many things.

Wayne McCarty was an unexpected ally. El had never expected Wayne to stand up to Bill Gunter. He better get hold of Otis or Henry and find out exactly how the vote had gone. Maybe he could work on a few of the no votes himself.

All at once, El chuckled to himself. He knew what he would preach on Sunday, Matthew 5:44: "Bless them that curse you, do good to them that hate you." He knew just where to start.

The sermon preparation went quickly; even though El worried periodically about Calvin. He wished the man would call. Should El call him?

El finished the first draft of his sermon before noon, so he went home for lunch. Holmes assumed that El's return meant a new serving of canned food. El disabused him of that idea although the kitten did sample El's sandwich meat.

After lunch, he decided he'd make some visits. A couple of members had entered the hospital, Randy Matsen for a hemorrhoid operation and Gladys Ferguson for treatment of her multiple sclerosis. Of course, they were at different hospitals. He decided to see the one furthest north first, Gladys in Seton Hospital.

The visit went well. Gladys was in good spirits, and the new treatment seemed to be helping. Gladys seemed more worried about him than herself. El appreciated that.

Next, El visited Randy who was more than a little embarrassed about being hospitalized for hemorrhoids. But El knew that Randy had had a heart valve replaced a few years back. Any operation could be risky. Randy's surgery had been early that morning and had gone well. Steve had sat with Randy's wife during the surgery. Randy was awake and in good spirits. His wife Louise was with him. El didn't stay long.

There was one last visit. Carol Hopkins was at home with a broken ankle. She was doing fine and expected to be back at work on Monday. So by four-thirty, El could head back to the office.

Martha looked more relaxed than she had that morning. The worry furrows had vanished. She smiled at El when he walked in. El nodded and went to his office. His eyes strayed to Calvin's file still on his desk. *Had Calvin gone to the sheriff?* If he didn't, what would El do?

As if in answer to his thoughts, Martha buzzed him to announce that Deputy Nelson was here.

The deputy strolled into his office. El didn't feel the hostility he'd sensed last time. Her eyes were almost friendly.

"Good afternoon, deputy. What can I do for you?"

"I need to know where you were last night from, say, nine on."

"May I ask why?"

The deputy smiled tightly. "You may, but right now I'd rather not tell you." She sat down in the chair nearest his desk.

El shrugged. Calvin must have gone to the sheriff, and the deputy was checking his story.

"I was home until about around ten-thirty. Calvin Roller called and wanted to talk to me. I'd called him earlier about church business, but he hadn't been in. We met at a local pizza place."

The deputy had opened her notebook and jotted down something as El spoke.

"We talked a while, then I went home. And so to bed."

Deputy Nelson cocked her head to one side. "What did you and Mr. Roller talk about?"

"I'm afraid I can't tell you. Mr. Roller came to me in confidence. I can't reveal our conversation. You'll have to ask him."

Deputy Nelson tapped her notebook on El's desk. "Can't. Mr. Roller was murdered last night. Probably on his way home from meeting you."

It was as if the floor had dropped away from El. The room around him suddenly seemed unreal. "Are you sure it was murder?" He barely kept himself from clutching his desk.

The deputy nodded. "It was. You want to tell me what Mr. Roller discussed with you now?"

El took a deep breath. "Of course." Why was the deputy waiting, why didn't she arrest him? *Why?* That must be the reason she was here. El suppressed the desire to get out of his chair and pace the room.

Briefly, El described his encounter with Calvin Roller. Deputy Nelson took notes, but did not interrupt. When he finished she leafed back through her notebook.

"You sure he didn't say who was the distributor?"

"I'm sure. Calvin said he didn't know, that Leroy made the contact. Do you think those men who kidnapped me might be the killers?"

"Might be. We don't know yet. Maybe the same person who killed Mr. Boyd, killed Mr. Roller. Don't worry though, we'll get 'em. Lieutenant Coronado's the best."

"That's good to know." El ignored the sinking feeling in his stomach. It would be so easy to pin both murders on him. He couldn't prove that he had gone home after his meeting with Calvin.

"Can I tell the rest of the staff about Calvin, Mr. Roller?"

"Sure, his wife's been notified."

Poor Edna, El thought. "When did you find him?"

"About noon. A couple of boys were riding their dirt

bikes in Pace Bend Park and found him. Still had his wallet. The medical examiner said he died about midnight.''

The deputy stood up. ''If you think of anything else, give us a call.'' She walked to the door, then turned and looked at El, her eyes hard. ''Don't do anything foolish. Be careful. These guys play for keeps.''

El could only nod. The warning surprised him. When she had turned El was sure she was going to arrest him after all, that the interview had been an elaborate ploy to get information before she read him his rights. *Why would the deputy think he might be in danger?*

El sat for a few minutes trying to sort out the events of the last two weeks. *Two deacons dead, both involved in drugs. The publicity had been bad before, what would it be like now?*

Publicity.

El punched the intercom button on his phone. ''Martha, get me Bill Gunter, then Wayne McCarty.''

''What's wrong, Pastor?''

El hesitated, but Martha had to know. ''Calvin Roller was killed last night. The deputy just told me.''

''Oh, no. In an accident?''

''No, he was murdered.''

After a short silence, Martha said, ''I'll call Bill Gunter.''

''Thanks.''

A minute later, El heard Bill Gunter's gruff hello. The man probably thought El was calling about last night's deacons' meeting.

El spoke bluntly. ''Brother Bill, I thought you would want to know that Calvin Roller was murdered last night and that it appears that he was Leroy Boyd's accomplice.''

''The hell you say,'' Gunter exploded, then, ''I'm sorry, Pastor. I didn't know Leroy, but I knew Calvin real well. He's not the kind to be mixed up in drugs.''

"I couldn't believe it either, but Calvin told me himself."

"Told you himself?"

"Yes." El gave the barest details of his conversation with Calvin. "He was killed soon after he talked to me."

"I see," Gunter said.

El could almost see his expression. What Bill Gunter meant was that El was the prime suspect.

Gunter went on, "I appreciate you telling me. If I can help Calvin's wife, let me know."

"Okay. Thanks."

"Good-bye."

Martha had Wayne McCarty on the line a minute later. The conversation was much the same. Finally, El said, "Maybe I better not go to Depew's tonight."

"Pastor, you need to go now more than ever."

"I don't know, Brother Wayne."

"I'll be by at eight." Wayne hung up.

After El put the receiver down, he was struck by the fact that both men saw Leroy as a drug dealer, but neither could conceive of Calvin as one. For that matter, neither could he. *Why had Calvin been killed?*

El decided he better see Edna. He told Martha where he was going and to be sure and pass the news on to Steve at home. After his early morning at the hospital, Steve had been in until noon, then taken the rest of the day off.

The Rollers lived in a small subdivision off of Pace Bend Park road, not one El had explored in his search for his kidnappers. El had been there for dinner only a few weeks ago. There were several cars in the drive when he arrived. El recognized Alice Taylor's. Edna Roller must have called her.

El knocked on the door, and Alice Taylor answered.

"Sister Alice, I'm glad you're here."

Alice Taylor smiled, but her eyes were unhappy. "I'm glad you came. Edna is awfully upset. Her sister is here and a neighbor, but she'll be relieved to see you.''

Alice Taylor showed El into the modest living room. Edna Roller sat on the sofa next to another woman who resembled her strongly, her sister, El assumed.

"Sister Edna, I'm very sorry about Calvin."

Edna Roller looked at him with red-rimmed eyes. "I knew something was wrong ever since Leroy died, but Cal wouldn't tell me." She sniffed, and her sister patted her hand. "When he got your message last night, he went all white. He never came back from seeing you."

El sat down in the chair next to Edna Roller. "I know. A deputy told me when it happened. If I'd known he was in danger, I'd never have let him go alone."

Edna wiped her eyes with a tissue and looked directly into El's eyes. "He was mixed up in drugs, wasn't he? Just like Leroy."

El could only nod.

"You knew. How?"

"I really didn't before last night," El said. "When I called I only wanted to see if Brother Calvin knew where the robe with pockets came from, but he thought I was on to him, so he told me everything."

Edna Roller looked away. "Drugs."

El searched for words of comfort. "He never meant to hurt anyone. Last night, he told me he was through with it. Maybe that's why he was killed. He was a good man that made a bad mistake. We all fall short."

Edna Roller nodded. "He was a good man."

El sat with her for a while longer then excused himself. Alice Taylor showed him to the door.

"I'd never thought our little church could hold such evil," she said.

"There's evil everywhere, Sister Alice, but also good. You just have to look. At least, it's over for us now."

"I hope so, Pastor, I hope so."

El went home instead of back to the office. He felt drained. As he pulled into his drive, he wondered why the deputy had not arrested him. From her sketch of Calvin's death, El had to be the prime suspect. He shook his head. It was probably just a matter of time.

"Dear Lord, is Calvin dead because of me? Oh, Lord, show me what to do."

▲19▼

EL WATCHED THE Channel 7 evening news to see if there was any mention of Calvin's death. There was only a brief report with no pictures and no mention of Hill Country Baptist Church. Relieved, El turned off the TV. Holmes was playing with his ball, again. He batted it across the room where it came to rest against the return vent for the air conditioning/heating. El watched him as he paused to examine the vent. The kitten ran his paws across the vanes of the vent a couple of times. It made a funny noise. Holmes cocked his head to one side and scraped the vent, again.

The sound reminded El of something. There had been a noise, not exactly like the one Holmes had made, but similar to it that night he had been kidnapped. Two of those strange sounds in a row not long before they reached the house, just like Holmes' scrapings. El identified the sound, a cattle guard crossing. The car had driven over two cattle guards in a row. Now, El remembered, he'd been surprised at the time. *How long between the cattle guards? Not long at all. There couldn't be that many places with two cattle guards in a row.*

El thought about calling Coronado. No, the lieutenant probably wouldn't think it significant. He'd wait until tomorrow. See if he still thought it worth telling. Besides, Wayne McCarty was coming by for him in an hour. El was glad they were taking separate cars. That way, after the party he could drive around awhile, maybe find that pair of cattle guards.

Wayne was right on time. He was dressed in slacks and knit shirt. El had adopted almost identical attire. At least it was an informal party.

"Hi there, Brother Wayne. I'm ready, but I'm still not sure I should be going."

Wayne grinned. "Sure you should go, just stay a little while. Maybe some of Depew's fundamentalism will rub off on you." Wayne's face grew solemn. "Calvin would understand. He voted to keep you at Hill Country."

Before El could answer, Wayne climbed into his car. Minutes later, El followed him left onto Highway 71. They went about twelve miles before Wayne signaled a left turn onto a road that El had not explored because it led away from Lake Travis. El pulled up behind him as Wayne waited for a break in the oncoming traffic. He had gone down the one on the other side of the highway. It had a cattle guard, but only one.

El went over more of his meanderings as he waited to turn. Then the highway was clear. He turned. Strange that Depew wouldn't be on the lake. A familiar whump startled him. A cattle guard. Now, if there was another. There wasn't. It wouldn't be that easy.

Suddenly, El realized it was that easy. Not two cattle guards in a row on the same road but one on either side of the highway. Just like here. Now that would give Coronado something to look for. There couldn't be too many places like that.

Wayne turned into a subdivision entrance. A large sign said Fair River Estates. El followed. The streets were wide and paved. From the distance between the first few houses they passed, the lots must be five to ten acres. The houses looked expensive, too. El couldn't keep from staring at each. Were any of these where he'd been held? Afterall, there had been two cattle guards.

El realized that he had slowed down. Wayne was almost out of sight. El speeded up to catch him. He'd look at these houses on the way out. They passed several more fine-looking homes. Dusk was just beginning to dim their outlines. Wayne slowed down, so El did, too. Ahead, to the left, was a broad, brightly lit drive lined with parked cars. The house must be set back far enough that it could not be seen from the street. Other cars were parked on the street. This was a large party.

Wayne pulled over and parked on the shoulder of the road behind a Lincoln. El pulled in behind Wayne. El noticed that the last car in the drive was a Jaguar. Depew had wealthy friends. El certainly didn't belong in such company. Why had he agreed to go to this party?

He caught up with Wayne at the foot of the drive. Wayne patted him on the back.

"It'll be okay, Pastor. Don't look so worried."

El nodded. "I'll try, Brother Wayne, I'll try."

They walked up in silence. El was trying, trying to come up with an excuse for leaving right now. All the cars they walked by looked expensive. Some makes El had never seen before, but there were plenty of Lincolns, Cadillacs, and Rolls Royces even. Wayne followed his gaze.

"Nice cars, huh?"

El nodded. This party was out of his league.

When they reached the front door, Wayne rang the bell. Inside, chimes rang. El studied the door, then glanced to his right.

"Good God," he said under his breath. His heartbeat quickened, and he fought the urge to turn and run. This was the house, the house where he had been held. He was sure of it.

"What's that, Pastor?" Wayne asked. His forehead slightly wrinkled. "Don't back out on me now."

El shook his head. Was he mistaken? Should he tell Wayne? Would Wayne just think El was crazy? *Matthew*

Marcus Depew's house, the kidnapper's house?

He had better get out of here. Drive home and call Coronado. Would Coronado believe him? Probably not. Probably think that El just found a likely looking house and made it up.

If El went in, he'd know for sure. The fear of that night caught at his throat. There shouldn't be any danger with all these guests. Besides, a man like Depew wouldn't be mixed up in drugs, not a zealot like him. El licked his lips. Maybe someone who worked with Depew was part of the drug ring. Maybe El better leave now.

At that moment, a tall, blond woman opened the door. She smiled at Wayne and him.

"Come in. No one's ringing the bell tonight."

The woman was breathtakingly beautiful. Her hair was piled on top of her head in loose swirls. Her eyes were a blue that reminded El of a clear summer sky. She smiled, a perfect smile, turned to her left, and walked away. Wayne and El followed. She had almost made him forget where he was.

El glanced to his left. There was his bathroom prison, its door open, just as immaculate. Wayne nudged El and winked, then gazed pointedly at the woman's hips. El frowned. He had to uphold a minister's image, even if a moment before he had been thinking the same thing.

Over her shoulder, the woman asked, "Are you friends of Mark's?"

"More friends of a friend, if you know what I mean," Wayne answered.

She laughed. "Indeed, I do."

El's stomach contracted as he followed the woman into the next room, the room where he had been questioned. The room did not look sinister, now, filled with people. A young woman sat in an overstuffed, blue-and-white-striped chair chatting with a young man perched on the arm. Was that the chair in which he had babbled his past away? And perhaps his future?

Two other chairs in blue and a love seat in white filled the area giving it a crisp, clean look. The folly of what he was doing suddenly hit him. *What if one of his kidnappers were here? What would he do?* Another thought came. *What connection did Depew have with the kidnappers?*

The woman drifted away without introducing herself. Wayne nudged El again. El jumped. He had forgotten Wayne.

"Want me to find Depew and introduce you?" Wayne asked.

"No, not just yet. You go on. Don't worry about me."

Wayne frowned a little as he looked at El. "You feeling all right? You look pale."

"I'm fine," El answered. Why didn't he tell Wayne? He just couldn't form the words. It would sound too crazy.

"Okay, but when you decide you want to meet the man, just find me."

El nodded. Wayne walked away weaving his way through the crowd. El studied the people. All were casually dressed, his own slacks and pullover shirt were standard attire for the men, although he doubted theirs came from the Sears Catalogue. The women were mostly in casual dresses, skirts, and blouses. Here and there one wore pants. El recognized no one, and no one seemed to be paying him any attention. Maybe the kidnappers weren't connected to Depew, maybe they had only used this house, maybe Depew had just rented it. *Maybe.*

El drifted toward the back of the room, along the way he picked up a drink. It looked like champagne. He sipped it. Ginger ale. He must have looked surprised because a man standing nearby grinned broadly.

"Mark doesn't believe in alcohol," the man said.

El nodded and moved away. He kept a lookout for short men. Shorty was the one man El thought he could recognize without his mask.

When El reached the back of the room, he realized he had underestimated the size of this house. The room was L-shaped, and he had entered the short leg. The long arm was three times bigger and opened onto a wide deck. More people filled both the room and the deck. No wonder there had been so many cars.

El edged out onto the deck. "So, I'm foolish, Lord. I just want to see if I recognize anyone. Then I'll get in touch with Coronado. I need something concrete to tell the Lieutenant," El said under his breath. There was one corner of the deck that was shadowed by a nearby tree, and he headed for it. Out of the light, he'd be safer.

Once there, he began to study the people around him. There was no sign of Wayne. Would he really recognize Shorty? A couple of men about ten feet away looked familiar. It took a moment for El to place them, then he knew. They were both State Representatives and three feet beyond them stood a State Senator.

El recognized another face and tried to withdraw further into the shadows. The man was a colleague of his, another Baptist minister, but from a larger, very conservative church. A couple of men strolled to the edge of the deck not far from him. One looked familiar, but El couldn't place him. The other was unknown. El eavesdropped on their conversation.

". . . The special session is almost over. What are you going to do when it is?" the unknown man asked.

The familiar one answered. "Well, the senator is keeping me on his staff here in Austin through January when the regular session begins. Then I'll be working for his committee during the session. And you?"

"I've got a job lined up with the state. It'll keep me

fed until Mark makes up his mind if he's going to run for governor.''

Mark? The man must be talking about Depew. *Dear Lord, if that man became governor . . .*

The familiar man shook his head. El tried desperately to place him. He was not one of the kidnappers. El was sure of that.

The familiar man spoke again. ''I don't think he should. He's carrying too much baggage because of his religion.''

''Come on, Baptists are the biggest religious group in Texas.''

''They also have the most enemies. Some people in his own denomination don't like him.''

The unknown man snorted, ''Left-wing skunks.''

''Those left-wing skunks vote.''

The man laughed. ''You're right.''

He said something else that El couldn't hear, then the men drifted away. As the familiar man half-turned toward him, El finally placed him. He'd been at the cemetery, at Leroy's funeral. The man in the cream suit. That didn't mean anything, did it? Just that he knew Leroy. Leroy had known lots of people, El thought, including drug dealers.

El resisted the desire to follow them. Maybe he should leave. The longer he stayed the more likely it was that one of his kidnappers, if they were here, would spot him. If one of them saw him before he saw them . . . El shivered although the only breeze was warm. He took a step toward the nearest door then stopped. He heard the voice. The voice that had questioned him that night. It was coming closer, out of the living room. El retreated into the shadows.

Three men stepped out onto the deck. El didn't recognize two of them, but he did the third, Marcus Matthew Depew, and Marcus Matthew Depew was the owner of the voice.

El almost dropped his ginger ale, he was so startled. The men walked by without even a glance in his direction. He couldn't distinguish the words, but every time Depew spoke, he saw the silhouette of his questioner looming over him. Depew was the one who had questioned him, had given the orders.

Good God, that man was a State Senator and a bulwark of the Southern Baptist Convention. No one would believe he was involved in drug dealing. No one. El shook his head. He must be mistaken. He'd heard the man on TV and not recognized his voice. No, there was a subtle difference that had not come through on the TV or radio. Depew was the head of a drug ring. Would Coronado believe him? It really didn't matter. El better get out of here.

He put his drink on the rail of the deck and sidled toward the door. He never took his eyes off Depew.

El made it into the living room without Depew seeing him. A minute later, El crunched down the drive as fast as he could. He kept looking over his shoulder. Knowing Depew was his kidnapper made him realize the folly of what he had done. If Depew had spotted him . . . El decided not to think about that.

All at once, he remembered Wayne. He should have told Wayne, gotten him to leave with him. No, wait. What if this were all a trick. What if Wayne was in it with Depew, Leroy and Calvin and had lured El here deliberately. That didn't make sense. Wayne couldn't be in on it, but it was too late, he wasn't going back into that house.

His car was just where he'd left it. He didn't know why he'd thought it might not be. He got in and tried to put the key in the ignition. He was shaking. The key wouldn't go in.

He took a deep breath, got the key in and started the car. Seconds later, he was on the road still headed away from the highway. There had been too many cars to turn easily, and he didn't want to call attention to himself. He drove a short way, then turned around and headed back. He slowed down as he passed Depew's home. No one seemed to have noticed his departure. He pressed on the gas and sped toward the highway.

"Dear Lord, what am I going to do? Will Coronado believe me? There's no telling who's on Depew's payroll."

▲20▼

S EL WAITED to turn onto 71, another car pulled up behind him. He glanced in the rearview mirror. The guy was awfully close. He couldn't see the driver, just a darker form inside the car. Whoever it was, their head was just above the steering wheel. El swallowed and his heart beat faster. Shorty was after him. Someone at Depew's must have spotted him. He had to get away quickly. An eighteen wheeler roared by on the highway. El hit the accelerator and pulled onto the highway right behind the truck. The other car followed.

Whoa now, don't let your imagination get the best of you, El said to himself. *It's probably just someone going home, too.* It was really too dark to be sure about the driver's height, the guy might be slouched down. El relaxed a little, then tensed again. He better be sure. There was a road to his left up ahead. El waited until he was almost to it, then he signaled and turned at the same time.

The other car turned, too, without a signal.

Fear returned. El's heart pounded. He speeded up and so did the other car. At least, it didn't try to gain on him. El had been up this road just the other day looking for the kidnapper's place. There was a circle drive two streets further. El turned into it. Again, the other car followed as if attached by a rope. Around the circle, then back on the street he'd just been on.

Soon, El could see the highway intersection. He'd head into town. At least there he'd have a chance. Suddenly, the other car accelerated and pulled along side blocking his chance to turn toward Austin. El could only see the driver's profile, but it was enough. The driver was Shorty.

El gunned the motor and turned toward the Pedernales, away from Austin. His old Mustang complained as he floored the gas pedal. El's hands slipped on the wheel. He wiped one then the other dry on his shirt. He glanced in the rearview mirror. Shorty was gaining.

The bridge was just ahead. Shorty could force him off it. To avoid that, El turned onto the Pace Bend Park road and once again floored the gas pedal. This was no road for high speed with its sharp twists and turns, but he had no choice.

El heard a popping noise. *What? Gunshots. Maybe.* They stopped. Nothing had hit his Mustang. The miles clicked by. Twice, El fought for control on a curve as the Mustang skidded perilously close to the guardrail. Luckily, the road was deserted, El could use both lanes. Shorty seemed content to hang back, perhaps planning to let the road finish El. The entrance to the county park was just ahead. El turned into the park with only a minimum of braking. Gravel hit the car as he slid sideways, but he kept control. There was a curfew on. Maybe a sheriff's patrol would pick them up.

To his surprise Shorty dropped back. El took a chance. He killed his lights just after he rounded a bend and made a hard left toward some large trees. He stopped. Shorty whizzed by and then was out of sight around the next turn.

El switched his lights on, backed out quickly, and headed out of the park. There was still no sign of Shorty when he reached the park entrance. What should he do?

The Paleface Park store at the intersection with 71 must have a phone. El headed back to the highway.

El pulled into the parking lot of the store. It was closed. He looked at his watch. After midnight. But El remembered the pay phones were outside on the far side of the building. He ran to them. A single light shone on both phones. There was a crude, hand-lettered sign on each phone: OUT OF ORDER.

El fought back the desire to scream at the phones. What was God's game? He ran back to his car and got in. Where to? Not home. The church probably had the nearest phone. El headed there.

Ten minutes later, he pulled into the drive. His headlights lit the parking lot. There were no other cars he saw with relief. He parked his car up next to the office. he already had his keys out by the time he reached the door.

He flipped on the light and stumbled to the phone on Martha's desk. He punched 911 and waited for the operator. He heard a car pull into the church drive. His grip on the phone tightened. *Please God, not Shorty.* The operator answered. The car's lights swept the office. El resisted the urge to drop the phone and run. He forced himself to speak.

"This is Eldon Lee Littlejohn. I'm at the Hill Country Baptist Church on Highway 71. There's someone after me. I think he plans to kill me. I can't talk anymore."

El didn't hear the dispatcher's reply. He put the receiver down on the desk. Maybe the open line could be traced, if the dispatcher had understood. He went to the front of the office and turned off the lights. With his back against the wall, he edged over to a window and looked out. Shorty was walking across the parking lot.

El took a deep breath. His heart raced. Think, he told himself. Think. Could Shorty know there was a back door to his office? Probably not. El locked the front door, then strode into his office, locked the office door behind him, then went out the back door.

Once outside, he paused to think. *Can I make it through the brush?* El studied the terrain. Over the years Harry had cleared the area pretty well. *If Shorty sees me, he'll have an easy shot. Dear Lord, what shall I do? I can't get to my car and can't stay here. I can at least get away from the back door. Lord, be with me.* El tiptoed to the corner of the building and looked around the corner.

Shorty rattled the front door, then stood back. He kicked it, the lock held. Shorty stepped back and pointed his gun at the door. He fired. The sound made El jump. Shorty kicked the door again. This time it gave. He went inside.

El drew back. He looked across the parking lot at the sanctuary. If he got there without Shorty seeing him, then the man might think El had taken off into the brush. El headed for the sanctuary in a low, crouched run. Halfway there, he heard what he thought was a muffled shot from inside the office building. He kept running. He reached the sanctuary door. There was no sign of his pursuer. He fumbled in his pocket for his keys. He got them and found the right key. He opened the door. As he did, a shot rang out. It hit the frame of the door above El's head sending splinters everywhere. One stung his cheek. He glanced over his shoulder. Shorty had come out the rear door of the office, just as he had.

El jumped into the sanctuary, slammed and locked the door. For a moment he stood there. What to do now? That lock would not stop Shorty for long. El looked around the sanctuary. There was really no place to hide. Should he go out the rear? Yes. He reached the main sanctuary doors. El once again fumbled with his keys. These doors required a key on either side. He inserted what he thought was the right key and turned it. The lock clicked. El tried to open the door. It didn't budge.

El tried again. No luck. The side door rattled. He had no more time to try.

El headed for the choir loft above the baptistry. It had two exits to the sanctuary. He could not be trapped there as long as Shorty was alone.

El reached the loft and crouched behind the organ to catch his breath and think. How long would it take the sheriff to arrive? That would depend on the location of the nearest deputy. He remembered all too well the TV reports showing the sheriff pleading for more deputies because their response time was too long. The sheriff hadn't gotten any more deputies. The county budget was too tight. El doubted that it would have made much difference to him. Any response time was going to be too long tonight.

"Dear Lord, be with me now. My soul is yours, if it be your will, my life, too. But I'd rather not die now Lord, if you don't mind."

A shot, more wood splintered. Shorty kicked in the side door of the sanctuary. El risked a peep around the organ. Yes, he could see him clearly in the outside light.

"Come on, Preacher, give it up. I'm going to find you anyway."

El pitched his voice to carry. With any luck Shorty would not be able to place it. "I've called the sheriff, leave while you have a chance."

Shorty cursed and turned toward the loft. "That's too bad Preacher, but I can't leave with you alive. This place will make a nice bonfire."

El scuttled to the other side of the loft closer to the stairs. His heart thudded and bitter taste filled his mouth. The man could burn the building down around him. Even if El escaped, the church would be destroyed.

"Why do you want to kill me?" Delay him, El thought. Give the sheriff time to get here.

Shorty laughed. "You know too much."

"I don't know anything." El answered.

Shorty gave a snort. "You know about Depew."

"I won't tell. Even if I did, no one would believe me."

"That Mex deputy would." Shorty's voice had changed. El realized he was coming closer to the choir loft.

"Looks like killing Baptists is getting to be a habit," he said with a funny little laugh that scared El more than his threats. "It's going to be a pleasure to blow your brains out. You shouldn't have killed Leroy. We were buddies from way back."

"I didn't kill Leroy," El said. "You guys questioned me. You know I didn't do it." How was he going to get out of this mess?

"Come on, Pastor, you passed out before the boss could ask that. But, we both know about the fight you and Leroy had. Threatened to make you leave here, I bet." El could hear Shorty walking slowly toward the choir loft. The vinyl tile under Shorty's feet crackled with each step. It needed to be reglued, but the deacons didn't want to spend the money. *Thank you, God, for cheapskates.*

El didn't ask how Depew knew about the fight. He looked at the steps out of the loft. He'd be a clear target going down as long as Shorty was on the sanctuary floor. El raised his head above the banister. Shorty was about twenty feet away.

"You'd better leave. The sheriff will be here any time."

Shorty headed toward El's end of the loft. Crouching, El scuttled to the other side. He'd go down as Shorty went up. Buy himself a little time.

Shorty leaped onto the bottom steps. El started down the others. Halfway down, his bad knee buckled. He tried to catch himself, but he was moving too fast. He fell and rolled to the foot of the steps. Before he could get up, Shorty appeared at the top, his gun pointed at El's chest.

El did not move. There was no escape now.

"Why not admit you killed Leroy?" El asked, stalling for time.

Shorty shook his head. "Cause I didn't, and if you didn't, then we're a murderer short." He chuckled.

El tried again. "But you did kill Calvin?" That must have been what Shorty meant about killing Baptists.

Shorty came down a step. He no longer looked short as he loomed above El. "Yep, just when I figured out who Leroy's cook was, he got religion. Your fault he said. You made him see the error of his ways. Too bad. By that time though he knew who I was. Couldn't let him live after that. He might have turned me in."

Poor Calvin. El had reached him, and it had cost him his life. But not his soul.

El had no more time for Calvin. He had to keep Shorty talking. "Why would a man like Depew be involved in drugs. He's got everything."

Shorty nodded. "So it seems. He does it for God." The man chuckled, "I do it for money. Lots of money. Depew takes the money, though. Says it's God's reward for his work. State Senators don't make a lot, even with the perks and the lobbyists, so we went big time a few years ago. It's going to be a hoot when he's governor and also the biggest drug distributor in Texas."

Shorty's answer had made his skin prickle. *What people did in God's name, Oh Lord.*

"How can he do it for God?" El asked Shorty, still stalling for time.

Shorty stretched out his arm, aiming. "You can ask God that."

El resisted the temptation to close his eyes. His heart thudded against his ribs. God. He'd die of fright before Shorty fired. All he could think of were Christ's words. "Into thine hands I deliver my spirit."

"Drop the gun, mister, you're under arrest." The voice came from the open door at the side of the sanctuary.

El twisted around to see. In the doorway was the chunky outline of Deputy Nelson, crouched slightly.

"Fuck you," Shorty shouted and swung his gun toward her.

The deputy fired and so did Shorty. The sound reverberated through the sanctuary. Then Shorty crumpled in slow motion on the steps of the loft. The deputy did not move.

El scrambled to his feet as Deputy Nelson walked toward him. She still had her gun out and pointed at Shorty's fallen form.

"Move out of the way, Preacher," she ordered.

El stepped down the steps and to the side. His knee complained but held. The deputy moved cautiously toward Shorty. His gun had fallen on the steps. She kicked it out of the way. She studied the fallen man, then holstered her gun and leaned over him. She put one hand on his neck. She shook her head.

"It looks like he's dead." She turned back to El. "You okay?"

El nodded. His knee still hurt, and his legs felt weak, but right now he was thankful to be alive. Deputy Nelson looked awfully pale. *Had she been shot?*

"How about you, Joyce?" He was proud of himself for remembering her first name. "Are you hit?"

She smiled weakly and pushed a stray strand of hair out of the way with a shaky hand. "No. He didn't get me. I never shot a man before, that's all."

"Oh," El had assumed that shootings like this were regular occurrences because she had acted so competently. "If you hadn't, I'd be dead."

Joyce laughed. "That's probably true. What did you do to make him want to kill you?"

"I found out who his boss was." Briefly, El explained

the evening's events and the chase. The only thing he left out was Shorty's denial of killing Leroy. El didn't know why, but somehow he thought that best.

"We'll have a heck of a time making a case against a guy like Depew."

El heard a siren wail. It was coming closer. For the first time, he realized that the deputy had arrived without one. That had probably saved his life.

Joyce looked at him. "Did you call them?"

"Yes, I mean, I thought you responded."

"No, I was looking for you. Coronado's had you under surveillance for the last week. That's why we knew you didn't kill Roller. I trailed you home from the pizza place." She shook her head. "I should have followed the other guy. I was supposed to have been on your tail this evening, too, but I got pulled off until about an hour ago. When you weren't home, I decided to check here. Lucky, huh?"

"Yes, but you know luck is just another name for God."

The deputy shook her head. "Mysterious are His ways, huh?"

El nodded.

Outside the siren stopped. El heard the sound of someone running. A man appeared in the doorway. "Don't anyone move," he said.

"It's all right, Billy. I've got it under control."

"Joyce?"

"Yes. Listen, get on the radio and send for the medical examiner. I just killed a guy."

"Sweet Jesus," the deputy said and turned away.

"It's going to get real complicated now. I wish there had been some other way."

El reached out and patted her on the shoulder. Somehow it seemed the right thing to do. "You had no choice."

"Guess not."

Deputy Nelson was correct. The next two hours were full of confusion for El. He was not sure how many times he told his story. He did remember Coronado's expression. A glint had come into the man's eyes that scared even El when he named Depew.

Coronado had allowed El to go to his office, but with orders not to call anyone. El wondered briefly who Coronado thought El would call at this time of night. The office was not in too bad a condition. The lock on his office door must have given way to one of Shorty's kicks, the door frame had splintered badly. The lock on his back door had been shot out. El managed to get it to close by propping a chair against it on the outside. Harry would have a lot of work to do in the morning. El sighed, after all this, the deacons would probably want him to pay for the damage.

No press had arrived. El was surprised at that. He glanced at the clock again as he had been doing for the last fifteen minutes. Two-thirty. No wonder he was sleepy.

There was a knock on the front office door, then it opened. Coronado walked in.

"Bad business, Pastor. Very bad." He looked at El as if seeing him for the first time.

Abruptly, he dropped into a chair. His dark eyes fastened on El's. "You want to help us clean this up?"

"Sure. Whatever I can do." El agreed without thinking.

Coronado looked away. "It might be dangerous."

El sat up, wide awake. "What do you want me to do?"

Coronado looked at him. "Go to Depew. Tell him you killed this guy. That you've changed your mind about making drugs. You're about to lose your job, anyway, and we're about to pin Leroy's murder on you. You need to move on. If he'll help you, then you'll make drugs for him."

He could only stare at Coronado. El was no under-cover agent. Depew would never buy such a story.

Coronado continued. "Tell him you want money now. Then set up the details of working for him."

Coronado looked expectantly at El.

"What if he just shoots me? He must have told Shorty to kill me."

"That's a chance you'll be taking, but I think I can give you an edge. I'm banking that he won't want blood-shed in his own home. We'll have you wired so we can record every word, and we'll be as close as we can. I won't lie to you, there is a lot of risk."

"Will Deputy Nelson be along?" For some reason, El wanted her there.

Coronado shook his head. "After a shooting, she'll be on administrative leave." He looked at El. "I can delay the report long enough for her to be with us, if that will make you feel better."

"It would."

"Okay." Coronado grinned. "She's first-class, you know."

El was taken aback by the glint in Coronado's eye. El didn't have that kind of interest in Deputy Nelson or did he? There was no time for that now.

"What's your exact plan?" El asked Coronado.

▲21▼

EL GULPED DOWN his third cup of coffee. He was still in his office. All the lights were on, and the room seemed glaringly bright. An hour had passed since Coronado had laid out his plan. As soon as Coronado got the equipment he needed, it would be up to El to make it work. El contemplated another cup of coffee. *Better not.*

Coronado had been in and out with Joyce Nelson. El was still surprised how comforting he found her presence. When this was over, he'd have to arrange something with her on a more informal basis.

El laughed at himself. Informal basis! What he wanted was a date with her.

Coronado came in with another man. "This is our electronics man. He'll fix you up."

Ten minutes later, El, wired for sound, was in his car headed back to Depew's house with Shorty's gun tucked in his belt. It wasn't loaded. Coronado hadn't liked that, but El had been firm. He wouldn't shoot anyone.

The drive and street in front of Depew's were no longer filled with parked cars. El drove up the drive and parked by the front door. He looked at his watch. Three-thirty. He got out of the car and glanced back down the drive. Coronado and Joyce stopped just past the drive entrance. El could not see their vehicle.

El pulled Shorty's gun from his belt, rang the door-bell, and waited. No one came. El rang the bell again. This time he heard a man's voice. *Depew?*

"I'm coming, I'm coming," he said.

The front door opened. Marcus Matthew Depew stood in the doorway in a plaid bathrobe. El wasn't surprised that Depew answered the door himself, Coronado had said the man lived alone. He had been married, but his wife had died many years ago. El had been surprised that a man like Depew didn't have a bodyguard or a live-in servant. El also worried that someone had stayed with Depew after the party, but it appeared Depew was alone.

"Move back." El shoved the gun into Depew's stom-ach and pushed him back into the hallway. He didn't want to give the man time to lock the door.

"What do you want?" Depew's voice had a hard-edged rasp that reminded El of the night he'd spent in this very room.

"I've changed my mind. I want to join your outfit," El said. "Or I want some big bucks to keep me quiet."

"I don't know what you're talking about. Get out of here before I call the police."

El poked Depew with the gun. He jumped.

"Don't tell me what to do. You sent Shorty to kill me because I figured out that you were Leroy's distrib-utor. But Shorty's dead, see, back at the church and I'm here." *Better be careful,* El thought. *Don't overdo the tough guy bit.*

Depew paled. "At the church? Who's Shorty? I . . ."

El stepped closer. "I said I know you're in charge. I want to have a cut. If you want, I'll cook your drugs. For the right money. I'll do a better job than Roller." He waved the gun in front of Depew's face.

The man's demeanor changed completely. "You didn't have to kill Al. If I'd known you wanted a cut,

I'd never have sent him. I figured you'd recognized me when I saw you leaving the party."

"I did, but I figured the party was no place for business, drug business. I didn't count on you setting me up," El said. "Just so you don't try to get me bumped off again, thinking you'll get away with it, I've fixed it so the sheriff will find out everything if I'm killed."

"I see." Depew stepped back. "Can we sit down?" Depew nodded toward the living room.

El wondered if it was a trick, but he nodded in return and followed Depew into the living room. Depew sat down in the easy chair. El decided to perch on the arm of the love seat.

"What's your deal. Pay me off or employ me?"

"Employ you. I need someone who can cook up stuff on demand, and maybe we can set you up in some church so we can launder our money. Leroy's death hurt us real bad."

"How much will you pay?" El asked. He really didn't know what else to say.

"That depends on how much dope you make and if you can help us with the money. You going to stay the pastor at Hill Country?"

El tried to snort derisively. "I'm already on my way out. Besides, I need to disappear. Remember Leroy?"

"So you did kill him."

El nodded. "I had a little fling with his wife. He didn't like it." El was glad that this story was Coronado's concoction, not his own. "That Sunday he wanted to talk to me after church. When I went back, I found him with the drugs. I guess I scared him. He grabbed his gun, we struggled, the gun went off."

Depew leaned back. "Why didn't you tell the sheriff the truth? It was self-defense."

"I was afraid that I'd lose my job. Even if Leroy was desecrating the church, my congregation might not believe the killing was justified. Besides, I might not have been believed, especially if it came out about Melanie and me. What then? I just didn't count on that lieutenant being so persistent.''

"For a greasy Messcan he sure is," Depew agreed.

El ignored the racial slur.

Depew studied him. El wondered if the man saw through his story. It was pretty thin. What had he told Depew the night he was questioned? Did it match what he was saying now? Shorty had said that they had not questioned him about the murder.

Depew leaned forward. His eyes narrowed. "You believe in the Bible?"

"Of course," El answered.

"You know what I mean. In the inerrant Word of God. From your preaching it's hard to tell. That's one of the reasons I agreed with Al that you needed killing."

El almost tipped off the arm of the love seat. The man was serious. A drug king who ordered a killing because of the inerrancy question. El swallowed. *God, forgive me for this lie.*

"I believe the Bible is without error, infallible."

"What about Adam and Eve?"

El tried not to giggle. There was something absurd about this conversation, but Depew was dead serious. *Emphasis on the dead, huh, Lord.* He knew the answer the man wanted.

"I believe that Adam and Eve were the first man and woman, that through them sin entered all of us. That they really lived. None of this evolution mumbo jumbo."

Depew visibly relaxed. "Damn right! Too bad I didn't know your feelings sooner. Your assistant seemed to think you were pretty liberal."

"Steve?" El felt sick. Steve had been reporting to this man? "He's the liberal. Told me himself, he thought women should be ordained. I told him no way. The Bible clearly says you have to be the husband of one wife. How can a woman be that?''

"You're so right. Well, I'll see he doesn't become pastor after you're gone.''

"Good. There is one other thing.''

"What?''

"The drugs. How do you reconcile selling drugs with the Bible? It's giving me some problems.''

"Good question. I'm glad you asked. Leroy understood, but Al never did. The people that use what I supply are sinners deserving eternal damnation. I'm just an instrument of God's judgment.''

El repressed a shudder. "How do you know?''

Depew leaned forward, his eyes gleamed with what El could only consider madness. "God spoke to me five years ago in December, just before Christmas. I was about broke. I told Him I was doing His work, that I needed money to continue it. How could I cleanse His House, if I was bankrupt? No one would respect me. Then He spoke to me. Told me there were lots of sinners out there deserving his wrath. I could deliver it.

"I already knew a little about the drug traffic in the state because of Al. I had hired him after he got out of jail as part of a rehabilitation program at my church for ex-cons. He'd been busted for making and dealing drugs. I went to him. Explained my vision. He was all for it. After that it was easy.''

"Easy?'' El's nervousness vanished. He was appalled by Depew's revelations. *All this in the name of God.*

"Sure, I've got contacts through the legislature. I made stopping drug dealers a personal crusade. Stamp out the competition. Got the Department of Public Safety more funding. In return, they kept me posted on their operations. I even went along on a few raids. Whenever the DPS busted a drug ring in an area, I moved in afterward.''

"So this wasn't your only operation?''

Depew shook his head. "I've got people working all over Texas and Mexico. Even in Lubbock," Depew chuckled. "The drugs Leroy supplied were just a little icing on the cake 'cause he found a chemist. He'd always had an idea that designer drugs would do well in a college town like Austin. He was right. I gave him an extra cut for that. Most of the stuff I handle comes from Mexico in return for money and construction equipment. That's another place where I'm really going to miss Leroy. He always picked out the equipment to steal, then held it at his yard until we could ship. No one noticed construction equipment among construction equipment."

He chuckled, then turned serious. His face lost expression, and El suddenly had the urge to run for the door.

"I always knew Al would come to a bad end," Depew said. "He didn't believe, you see."

"Didn't believe?"

"In my mission. He said I was crazy. That this was just a good way to make money, that's all. You see what happened to him. God knows what's in your heart."

"That's true," El agreed. "Such people condemn themselves by their own actions. I understand now, you're just helping God."

Depew nodded. "Only another man of God could understand. But if you work for me, you must not commit adultery again. I won't have it."

Again, El had the desire to giggle. *No sex, just drugs.* "You're right. I've already confessed to God and asked His forgiveness."

"Good," Depew said. "I've got an idea."

El watched him warily. Had this talk all been fake to throw him off guard?

"Where's Al's body?" Depew asked.

"Back at the church. Why?"

Depew's eyes took on a dreamy look. "Let Al take

the blame for Leroy's murder. He would have killed him someday. Al kept saying that Leroy was keeping some of the dope he got from the sales in Mexico. Leroy was the one that put a price on the heavy equipment. Al thought we should be getting more for that big stuff than we were. When Leroy turned up dead, I figured Al caught him shorting us and killed him. Just wouldn't admit it to me.'' Depew's gaze sharpened. "You go back to where you left Al's body."

El shook his head. "The sheriff will want to know why I waited to call him."

Depew grinned. "That's easy. Al chased you. You struggled for the gun, it went off, killing him. You were shocked by that. You just sat in the church until you finally came to yourself. Then you called the sheriff. After all, a man of God should be stunned by that."

"It might work."

"It'll work. I'll see that some stuff is planted at Al's apartment that links him to Leroy. You can say he admitted killing Leroy."

"Sounds okay. How do I know that you won't double-cross me?" El asked.

Depew scowled at him. "I keep my word."

El said nothing.

"I swear before the Almighty that I'll not betray you."

El nodded. "I believe that."

"Good. Now get back to the church and call the sheriff."

El stood up, but he kept the gun on Depew. "I don't want to stay at Hill Country even if this works."

"You won't have to. How about a church in East Texas, in the Piney Woods? I got a farm where you can make the stuff. We're already making some speed there and using the church to clean up some of our East Texas money. The preacher isn't in on our deal. I'll find him another church and move you in there. Then we can really push the money through. I can arrange for you to live nearby.''

"Maybe. I'll have to pray about a move like that. You'd want me to make that synthetic heroin like Roller did?''

"Sure, only more. I can distribute it in Houston as well as Austin. If you make enough, I can move some in New Mexico as well as the rest of Texas.''

"New Mexico?'' El didn't have to fake his surprise. "You go that far? How do you keep track of everything?''

Depew grinned. "We've just moved into New Mexico in the last six months. This is a big operation, boy. I'm computerized. Everything's on my PC. Dealers. Buyers. Chemists. Delivery times. The whole works. Come on, just follow me.''

El hesitated. Was Depew trying to trick him?

"Aw, come on.'' Depew must have sensed El's unease. "Just in my office across the hall.'' Depew indicated the entry hall.

El nodded. "Lead the way.''

Depew led him across the hall to another room, obviously Depew's office. A microcomputer, printer, and other peripherals sat on a desk against the far wall. Depew headed for it.

"That where you keep the info?''

"No, of course not. Too dangerous, but I can access the one that does. Hold on.''

Depew sat down in front of the computer. He typed some commands and the computer beeped. He leaned back and looked at El. The man seemed completely relaxed.

"Just waiting for it to call the other one.''

El nodded as if he understood.

The computer beeped again. Depew leaned forward and typed again. The computer screen cleared, and a map of Texas appeared.

"Now, look. Those red dots are where I've got distribution centers, the green are receiving points, and the yellow are where we cook up some stuff. Look over here."

Depew pointed to a yellow spot in East Texas. "That's where you'd be going."

"I see," El said. "Isn't this dangerous? All this information on your computer. I mean, you're not home all the time."

Depew's grin widened. "I told you, none of this is saved here. This is stuff on my computer down at the capitol. No one's going to get into that. When I switch off here, nothing is saved. My senate staffers are all in on the deal. They understand the mission we're on. Remember, I've got God on my side."

"Oh," El wondered if that was enough for Coronado. He hoped so because he wanted to get away from Depew. The man made him feel unclean. "If I'm going to make this work, I'd better get back to the church." El took a step toward the door.

"It'll work." Depew stood up and followed El as he walked to the door. "Don't you worry, boy. I'll get everything set. You just relax until then. Okay?"

"Well," El said, but before he could say more Depew reached into his robe pocket and swung something at him. El tried to duck, but the man was fast. El's world dissolved in pain and darkness.

El heard voices. He wished they would shut up so he could sleep. Someone said, "He's coming around."

El opened his eyes. A stranger was looking him in the face. The stranger had a uniform on and a necklace around his neck. Not a necklace, a stethoscope. The man was a paramedic. El felt proud of his reasoning powers. Now, if he could just go back to sleep.

"Don't go to sleep on us just yet, Reverend." The

man took out a small light and pointed it into El's eyes. "We're taking you to the hospital."

El could only stare at the man. This was a dream, no a memory. He'd done this last week. El tried to sit up. He couldn't. Someone had tied him down. He raised his head to see. The whole side of his head throbbed. He dropped it back.

This wasn't last week. He remembered. *Depew*. The man had sworn before God and still tried to kill El. There were voices to his left. El turned his head carefully. Maybe he could see what was going. He was still in Depew's house, in the front hallway. The paramedic had returned with Coronado.

Coronado's left arm was in a sling, but he grinned at El. "We got him."

The paramedic frowned at Coronado. "You should be on a stretcher, too."

Coronado shook his head. "No way. One's enough. How's the head, Reverend?"

El raised his eyebrows. "I can't tell. What happened?"

"I bet you'd like to know." Coronado stepped closer, but the paramedics were moving El. "I'll ride along with you. These guys want me to anyway." One of the paramedics snorted derisively.

To El's surprise his head didn't hurt as he was loaded into the ambulance. One of the paramedics helped Coronado in. He looked pale, but he grinned at El as he sat down.

As soon as they started moving, El looked expectantly at him.

"Okay," Coronado said. "We heard everything. When he hit you, we came on in. It was probably my fault."

"Your fault?"

"Yes, as we ran up the drive, we could hear him after he hit you. He kept babbling, 'Adulterer, Adulterer.' I'm sorry, Reverend. When I set you up with that story about Mrs. Boyd, I didn't expect that."

El grinned at Coronado. "Neither did I."

Coronado gave a short sigh. "Well, we broke down the door. Depew was dragging you toward the back. He looked like a cat caught on the dining-room table. Tried to put it all on you. He went berserk when I told him you'd been wired. He had a gun. That's what he hit you with, I think."

"And shot you?"

"Yeah, it happened too fast. I was careless. You're not the only one who owes Joyce your life. She knocked the gun aside, otherwise the bullet would have been in my chest. Disarmed him, too." Coronado shook his head. "I'll have to see if she'd like to work homicide."

"What's going to happen now?"

"Well, Depew's on his way to jail, and the feds, the Austin Police, and someone from my office are on their way to the Capitol. The next few days are going to be real interesting." Coronado leaned back and closed his eyes.

El had more questions, but he did not disturb Coronado. The rest of the ride was in silence. It wasn't long before the same emergency-room doctor from last week was examining El.

"You're more than lucky. Two head injuries and neither serious, but this time you've got a concussion for sure. You'll have to stay in the hospital for at least a day."

El decided not to argue, besides he was not sure he could. He was too sleepy. Instead, he yawned in the doctor's face. "Sorry, I've been up all night."

"I gathered that. We'll get you a room in a few minutes. Until then just relax. Sleep if you want to."

El nodded slightly. He wanted to sleep. He'd just closed his eyes when someone said, "Sorry, Reverend, need to talk."

El forced his eyes open. It was Coronado again.

"You can't tell anyone what happened for a day or two. We need to round up the gang. You understand."

"Yes," El said.

"Good. Just tell your family and friends that you were helping us all along. We'll make sure they know you're the good guy. But don't give them any details. Right?"

"Right," El echoed. Coronado didn't need to worry about El talking to anyone. He was going to sleep for the whole weekend. Starting now. El closed his eyes.

▲22▼

EL OPENED HIS eyes. His mother smiled at him. El smiled back.

"I'll get up in a minute, Mom," he said and closed his eyes. He'd just get a little more sleep before school.

El opened his eyes again. *I'm not in school anymore. Haven't been for years. What is my mother doing here? Where is here?* El remembered. *The hospital, then Shorty, Depew, and the rest. What a night.*

He smiled at his mother, again. She looked worried. Her lips pressed together in a thin line, and her eyes glittered with unshed tears.

"Don't look so worried," El said. He looked past her. His father hovered just behind her. Why were they so concerned? He had just needed some sleep. From the way he felt he had slept hard, too.

"We should be worried," his mother said. His father nodded vigorously.

"How'd you find out I was here?" El did not remember telling anyone to contact his parents or . . . *Dear Lord! The church.* He hadn't told anyone at church. He would have to call Steve.

His mother patted his shoulder apparently oblivious to his consternation. "The sheriff, himself, called us. Told us that you were in the hospital. He also said you're a hero, but no details." His mother shook her head.

"What happened?" his father asked, leaning forward.

El opened his mouth to tell him, then remembered Coronado's admonition. "I can't tell you yet. The investigation is still going on."

His mother frowned. She was trying to look stern. He'd never seen her succeed. She didn't now.

"Really, Mom, I can't tell."

"Okay, but at least tell us how you got hurt."

"I think I can do that, but first you've got to call the church for me and tell them that I can't preach on Sunday."

His mother's eyes widened. "What day do you think this is?" she asked.

"Saturday."

"It's Sunday. You've been asleep since Saturday morning."

El stared at his mother's blue eyes. She wouldn't kid him. He'd lost a whole day.

"Then the church knows."

Both his parents nodded. "Steve Forbes has been here most of the time. He'd be here now except for morning services. It's ten-thirty."

El relaxed. At least the church was taken care of. "How did Steve find out?"

"Same as us. The sheriff. He wanted to make it very clear what a great help you'd been and how innocent." His father grunted, then continued. "I thought he was a little over enthusiastic about your innocence. Someone must have had some doubts at one time."

El nodded and got the first reminder of his escapade yesterday. His head throbbed dully. He lay back.

His mother immediately reached out to touch his arm. "You okay?"

"I'm fine. I'll tell you what I can of what happened." Briefly, El outlined the events leading up to his injury only leaving out names. He started with his discovery that the party he was attending was in his kidnapper's house. When he finished, his parents stared at him. He couldn't keep from chuckling. Both were round-eyed and open-mouthed.

"It's not funny," his dad said gruffly. "You could have been killed. I hope you never get involved in something like this again."

El grinned. "Dad, I guarantee I'm not going to do something like this again." El looked out the window. It was a fine morning. Suddenly, he shivered as if he had stepped through an August thunderstorm, chilled on a hot day. He had forgotten his new housemate.

"What's wrong?" his mother asked immediately.

"My cat. I told you I got a new cat. I forgot him. He hasn't been fed since Friday."

His mother sighed and smiled indulgently. "Well, I didn't forget him. I brought him home with me. He didn't want to be alone way out in the country. He's really enjoying himself."

"He's my cat," said El, emphasizing the *my*. His mother loved anything with fur or feathers. She'd have no qualms about making room for Holmes permanently.

His mother's smile broadened and she patted his shoulder. "You rest. When you go home, you can get him."

Behind her, his father's head made quick, jerky nods. His dad liked animals, but not to the extent his mother did. Because of her, he tolerated a household of two dogs, three cats, and a parakeet. El knew he didn't want a fourth cat.

"All right," El said.

A nurse came in. El noticed that her brown hair was done up in a bun on top of her head. It reminded him of something, but he couldn't quite recall what.

"Well, you're awake at last," the nurse said. She checked his pulse and stuck a thermometer in his mouth, one of the new kind attached to a small box.

El noticed one hairpin stuck out slightly as she leaned

over him. He looked at it closely, still trying to recall what its significance was.

"Very good," the nurse said when she finished. "Feel like some breakfast?"

El realized he was ravenous. "Yes," he said.

"Good," the nurse said, reaching over and plumping his pillow. "I'll have a tray sent up." She smiled and left.

The tray arrived within five minutes. While El ate, he chatted with his parents. He stopped eating when his father told him that they had maintained an around-the-clock vigil at his bedside.

"Around the clock?"

"Of course, dear," his mother answered. "Your dad took the eleven to seven shift last night. I came at seven, but he decided to stay a while."

"Your mother was here with you all day Saturday," his father added.

"Well," El said, "You both go home now. Get some rest. I'm going to be fine. Look, I've eaten everything in sight."

His mother looked uncertain, but his dad nodded. "I think he's right, hon. We'll come back this afternoon."

"I'm not sure we should leave you. I'll stay," his mother said.

El shook his head. "No way, Mom. Go home."

His mother nodded reluctantly. With his father providing some needed prodding, El finally got her to go. After they left, he leaned back and closed his eyes. What an adventure. *Thank you, Lord, for getting me through it.*

The nurse returned and took away the tray after complimenting him on his appetite. El smiled at her. She was not bad-looking.

Depew. What would his arrest do in Baptist circles? In the legislature? The man had been a power. What if he had gotten to be governor? Well, it wouldn't happen now.

Something else bothered El. It was like an old sting that kept itching. *What was it?* Then El remembered. *I hadn't told Coronado what Shorty had said about not killing Leroy.* He should have, but somehow he'd been reluctant to. *Why?*

Because he had believed Shorty when he said he didn't kill Leroy, and if he hadn't done it, then someone else had. Someone else had set all this in motion by killing Leroy. *Someone in the church?*

No. That was ridiculous. But who else but a church member could have come and gone without being noticed? A stranger or visitor hanging around after church would have been remembered unless they came after everyone left. How could somebody time that?

He had always assumed that the killing was drug connected. *What if it were not?*

Who had been the last to see Leroy that day? El didn't know. Nobody came to mind. Think of a different approach to the problem. Who had seemed different after Leroy's death? Now, maybe that was the way to go. El stared out the window, letting his mind go blank. Still no one came to mind.

Harry had found that hairpin. Now, El knew what he was trying to remember when the nurse had been in. El had never given that hairpin to Coronado. A nice, sturdy hairpin, not like the nurse's thin one. Probably belonged to one of the girls he baptized that day, but he didn't remember either of them having their hair up or even pinned.

He tried to picture the activities of the day. That Sunday had not been extraordinary; baptisms took place every eight to ten weeks.

Who had killed Leroy? Who had set this all in motion? Who?

El went through the baptisms. El chuckled to himself

remembering Tom Rivers. Otis Wheeler had helped on the men's side. Alice Taylor had helped on the girl's side. Bless Sister Alice.

Suddenly, El's stomach jumped, and he sat up. He knew who had killed Leroy. It was obvious, but why hadn't the shooter come forward. It must have been in self-defense. As soon as he was out of here, he had to have a talk with that person.

"Dear Lord, help me to choose the right thing to do. I need your strength and wisdom. Amen."

El finished his lunch. He had been hungry again despite the earlier breakfast tray. Since his parents left, he had gotten up once with the help of the nurse. He'd used the facilities under her supervision. When he was back in bed, she fluffed his pillow and smiled at him.

"Don't get up by yourself. That's doctor's orders. Okay?"

El nodded obediently, but he had his mental fingers crossed.

El pushed his tray table away and leaned back. He stared out the window at the parking garage next door. He was just beginning to feel bored when someone said "Good afternoon, Reverend."

In the doorway stood Coronado. He looked the same as usual except for a dark blue sling cradling his left arm. He smiled lazily.

"I wanted to thank you again," Coronado said. "Yesterday morning, I had the feeling you were sort of out of it by the time I finished."

El grinned back at Coronado. "Sort of is an understatement. I just woke up this morning. Gave my parents a scare."

"Us, too, Reverend. I left orders for the hospital to call me as soon as you woke up. When they didn't call yesterday, I phoned them. The doctor seemed sure you were okay, but you were asleep a long time." Coronado shook his head. "I thought maybe Depew had done more damage than the doctor first thought. I wouldn't want to lose you. You make a pretty good undercover agent."

"Not very good, I didn't have sense to see what a liar Depew was. I believed that I'd convinced him."

Coronado chuckled. "I think that was the problem. You did convince him, convinced him you were an adulterer." Coronado shook his head. "He's confessed to everything, naming all his accomplices, and that computer of his, boy, we hit the jackpot. But he asked about you. Wanted to know about you and Mrs. Boyd. He was real relieved to find out you weren't having an affair with her. Told us he 'couldn't abide the thought of a minister committing adultery.' I swear he seemed almost happy when we told him it was all made up just to get him."

El could only shake his head. Depew had to be mad.

Thinking of Depew, El remembered Shorty's pursuit. It seemed somehow unreal now.

"I'd never had a chance to be an undercover agent if you hadn't had Joyce Nelson watching me."

Coronado shrugged. "I always figured you were the key. That eventually whoever shot Leroy would come to you. I didn't count on another murder though, but we got the man that killed them both, thanks to you and Deputy Nelson."

El said nothing.

Coronado shook his head. "I never expected to bust the whole drug operation. It was big. Depew had ranches and farms all over the state. He manufactured speed and stored other drugs and stolen heavy equipment at those places. He used the heavy equipment to pay for more drugs in Mexico. Quite an operation. All I can say is thanks, Reverend." Coronado held out his hand.

El shook it gladly. This was the first time the detective had offered his hand. His grasp was firm and friendly.

"Good day, Reverend."

"Good day, Lieutenant."

"Oh, by the way, you can tell people what happened. No secrets now." Coronado said from the door.

El nodded.

El's doctor came a little later. He was reassuring, but he wouldn't let El go home until the next day.

The telephone rang just as the door closed behind the doctor. It was Wayne McCarty.

"Hi there, Pastor. How are you feeling?"

"Pretty good, Brother Wayne. Pretty good."

"Pastor, what happened Friday night?"

Briefly, El explained.

"Why didn't you tell me you recognized that house?" Wayne asked.

"Brother Wayne, to tell the truth, I don't know. I guess I was so surprised, I didn't think."

"Just so you didn't think I was part of this drug ring."

"No, I never thought that," El said. He didn't want to hurt Wayne's feelings. Besides, he had decided Wayne wasn't part of the gang. That still didn't explain why he had not turned to Wayne for help. He really didn't know.

Wayne laughed. "Good. But, that's not why I called. The deacons sort of met informally right after church today. You can forget about leaving Hill Country. Everyone wants you to stay. Some of the guys are pretty embarrassed, especially when they found out you had been helping the sheriff all along. I hope they have the nerve to apologize to you face to face. Well, anyway, that's it. You're the Pastor."

"Thanks, Brother Wayne. I appreciate hearing that. I want to thank you for going to bat for me earlier."

"Pastor, it was the least I could do."

"Brother Wayne, what about Bill Gunter. What's he saying?"

There was silence at the other end of the line. El wondered what Gunter had been up to that could silence Wayne. He started to tell Wayne never mind when he spoke.

"I was going to wait till you were out of the hospital to tell you. No one else knows, yet, not even Reverend Forbes."

El suppressed the urge to tell Wayne to spit it out, instead he waited.

"Pastor, Bill Gunter's leaving the church. Says there's not room for you and him both, that you have a different vision. I just think he knows when he's beat. I say good riddance."

"He's leaving the church," El repeated. He could not believe that Gunter would do that. "He was one of the founders, Brother Wayne."

"Yeah, I know, but I always thought he just tagged along with those who really had a vision. Oh, Brother El, I shouldn't have said that. You won't repeat it, will you?"

"Never, Wayne, never."

"Good, I think I've kept you long enough. Take care. Good-bye."

"Good-bye."

El put the receiver down and lay back. *Bill Gunter was leaving. Miracles did happen.* El could stay at Hill Country, but did he want to? He didn't know.

"Dear Lord, what shall I do?" He closed his eyes to think.

El must have dozed again. A knock on the door woke him. *Good Lord, am I going to sleep my life away?*

"Come in," El said. He glanced at the clock. One-thirty. Steve Forbes walked in, grinning.

"Good to see you awake. We missed you in church this morning. We had a pretty good turnout, but I didn't get a chance to count."

"What about the offering?" El asked. Summer was

always a rough time financially for the church. When people went on vacation, so did their giving. The church always spent the fall catching up.

"Pretty good for the middle of the month."

"That's a relief. I was afraid with all that was going on that we'd see a real drop."

"No, I think it's up, thanks to you. When Coronado called and told me you'd been part of the plan from the beginning, I made sure the deacons knew right away. The news spread fast." Steve grinned. "Martha helped it along considerably. She came in Saturday afternoon and called people. A lot of people decided they better start coming to church. I think some were there just hoping to see you. They were disappointed this morning, but wait till you are back."

"Did you tell them I was just sleeping it off?"

"I'd never say that," Steve responded in a shocked tone.

El sighed. When would he ever learn that Steve couldn't take a joke? "I know, I just meant that you assured them I wasn't in too bad of shape."

"Oh, I see. I did that. I expect some will drop by to see you, although I told them I didn't know if you would be up to visitors." Steve looked at El hard.

"I'm doing fine. The doctor says it's more exhaustion than anything else."

"That's good." Steve said.

Neither said anything for a moment. El contemplated Coronado's embellishment of his role. He'd made the church think that El was never a suspect. What would Coronado say if he knew that El was withholding a murderer's identity?

"El," Steve said.

With difficulty, El focused on him. "Yes."

"I did something you should know about."

"I think I know," El said. "You talked to Depew and

Gunter about me, hoping that if I left, you'd get my job. How did you meet Depew?''

Steve actually paled. "I never met him, I only talked to Brother Boyd and Brother Gunter. I'm sorry, El. Do you want me to resign?"

"No, Steve, it's all right. We all have ambitions. We just have to make sure we keep perspective. After things settle down, we'll have a long talk."

"Thanks, I'd like that." Steve stood. "I better get going. You won't be alone, I'm sure. Bye."

"Bye, Steve."

After he left, El thought about the future. Should he have taken Steve up on his offer to resign? Should he let Steve stay and he go? Maybe he just wasn't cut out to be a minister or at least a Baptist minister.

"Dear Lord, what shall I do," El said. Boy, had he been asking that a lot lately. He closed his eyes to pray. A light tap on the door interrupted his prayer. Alice Taylor peeked around the door.

"Sister Alice, I'm glad to see you."

Alice Taylor smiled in return, but her face quickly grew serious. "The nurse said you were awake and could have visitors, but I won't stay if you don't feel up to it."

"I'm fine," El said and hitched himself up in bed. "Sit down. We had an appointment anyway."

"I know," Alice Taylor said. "That's really why I came. Pastor, I've something awful to tell you."

El looked at the woman's lined face and worried eyes. "You don't have to, I know."

Alice Taylor's eyebrows went up and she cocked her head to one side. "Do you?"

"Yes. Harry found a hairpin in the baptistry. It's yours, I believe. It fell there when you struggled with Brother Leroy." El paused. "And killed him."

Alice Taylor came over and sat down in the chair next

to the bed. She nodded slowly. "I didn't know that I lost one."

"Why didn't you tell someone what happened?" El asked. That was really the puzzle.

Alice Taylor bowed her head. "I was so ashamed. To shoot someone in God's house."

"But it was self-defense."

"Yes, I suppose so."

El waited, but she did not continue. He prompted her. "You went back to give Leroy your offering because you had been helping the girls who'd been baptized when the plate was passed."

"That's right. I could have mailed it or waited until next Sunday, but I knew Leroy counted the money right after church, so I went back to give him my check. I stopped to visit with Thelma, so it was a while before I got back there.

"I was afraid I'd missed him. There was no one at the counting table, but the money bag was on the table. I thought he must be in the rest room, so I put my check in the bag. I was thinking about leaving him a note when I saw his gun in the chair. To think he'd brought a gun into the church, I was shocked. I picked it up."

El could imagine how irate Alice Taylor had been, and with her upbringing there would be no fear of a gun, just anger.

"Right then, Leroy came out from the dressing area. He had two little packages in his hand. He stopped when he saw me. He looked so surprised.

" 'Sister Alice, how can I help you,' he said, then he must of noticed that I had his gun. 'I'm sorry about the gun. I was afraid to leave it in my car. The lock on the door is busted.'

" 'What's in those bags?' I asked him.

" 'Nothing,' he said.

"But I was suspicious. I said, 'I think we better talk to the pastor.'

"He got real mean then. Threatened me, even though I still had his gun. He grabbed for me, but I was too quick. I surprised him, I think. He didn't expect an old woman to move like I did. I told him to stay back or I'd shoot. He did for the moment. I started to leave, but he followed me. When we got to the stage he sort of lunged at me. His hand brushed my head. I shot him, and he fell in the baptistry. I waited, but no one came."

"Why didn't you call someone?" El asked.

Alice Taylor shook her head. "I'm a good shot. I knew he was dead. When I realized no one had heard the shot, I just wanted to get away. I just couldn't face the thought of everyone knowing what I'd done. He'd dropped the packets when he went for me. I picked them up, I didn't want them to fall into the wrong hands. I figured they were drugs of some kind. Still, no one came, so I left. There was no one in the parking lot when I got outside. I saw Harry had been cleaning around the arborvitae, so I pushed the gun into the ground under the nearest one. Harry does a good job, the soil was soft way down. Then I went straight home."

She looked at El. "I'd never have let you take the blame, but I just didn't know what to do. I didn't want you to go to jail. I knew you were innocent, so I figured God would protect you."

Alice blinked away tears for a moment. "That man did need killing. He abused his wife and kids. I almost didn't come to sit with Melanie that day you called, but I'm glad I did. I found out what a terrible man Leroy was." Alice shook her head. "Then when all the other stuff started happening with you getting kidnapped, escaping and all, I decided I better talk to you. Tell you the truth."

"God did protect me, Sister Alice, he did. What happened to those packages of Leroy's?"

"Oh, I took them home and flushed the powder down the toilet." She shook her head. "It killed the yeast in my septic tank, you know. I had to have the darn thing pumped out.''

El smiled. ''I imagine that stuff would.''

Alice Taylor bowed her head. ''If I had come forward right away, poor Brother Calvin would still be alive. None of this would have happened.''

El reached out and took her hand. ''What you did, let the sheriff clean up one of the biggest drug syndicates in the state. You have nothing to be ashamed of.''

''I'll tell the sheriff.''

''You can if you want to, but they think that the bad guy that the deputy killed was the one who shot Leroy. I see no harm in letting them think that. He had killed other men.'' El remembered Calvin. ''No one need ever know that you killed Leroy Boyd.''

Alice Taylor dabbed at her eyes with a hankie. ''If it just hadn't been in church. I just can't face people knowing I shot a man in church.''

''You don't have to.''

Alice Taylor looked at El and squeezed his hand. ''Thank you.''

She left.

El got out of bed and gingerly moved to the chair. All this because she was ashamed of killing a man in church.

''Dear Lord, I hope what I just did was right. She's an old woman. She doesn't need to be hurt.''

El sat in silence for a moment, then continued. ''Thank you, Lord, for this congregation. Let me be a good shepherd to it. Amen.''

El sighed. He guessed he had his answer. He'd stay with the church a while longer. It did seem to be God's will.

FAST-PACED MYSTERIES
BY J.A. JANCE

Featuring J.P. Beaumont

UNTIL PROVEN GUILTY	89638-9/$4.99 US/$5.99 CAN
INJUSTICE FOR ALL	89641-9/$4.50 US/$5.50 CAN
TRIAL BY FURY	75138-0/$4.99 US/$5.99 CAN
TAKING THE FIFTH	75139-9/$5.50 US/$7.50 CAN
IMPROBABLE CAUSE	75412-6/$4.99 US/$5.99 CAN
A MORE PERFECT UNION	75413-4/$4.99 US/$5.99 CAN
DISMISSED WITH PREJUDICE	
	75547-5/$4.99 US/$5.99 CAN
MINOR IN POSSESSION	75546-7/$5.50 US/$7.50 CAN
PAYMENT IN KIND	75836-9/$4.99 US/$5.99 CAN
WITHOUT DUE PROCESS	75837-7/$5.50 US/$7.50 CAN
FAILURE TO APPEAR	75839-3/$5.50 US/$6.50 CAN

Featuring Joanna Brady

DESERT HEAT	76545-4/$4.99 US/$5.99 CAN
TOMBSTONE COURAGE	76546-2/$5.99 US/$6.99 CAN